INSIDE

Also available by J.A. Jarman

Hangman

Ghost Writer

Peace Weavers

INSIDE

J.A. JARMAN

Andersen Press
London

First published in 2010 by
Andersen Press Limited
20 Vauxhall Bridge Road
London SW1V 2SA
www.andersenpress.co.uk
www.juliajarman.com

British Library Cataloguing in Publication Data available.

ISBN 978 184 270 977 1

Typeset by Palimpsest Book Production Limited,
Grangemouth, Stirlingshire

Printed and bound in Great Britain by
CPI Bookmarque, Croydon CR0 4TD

For Julie Laslett

CHAPTER 1

'Open your mouth.'

I looked around.

'You, Mercer! I'm an officer. Open your mouth.'

Officer? Not police. Wrong uniform. Dark blue.

He stuck his fat face in front of mine.

'Look left.' He peered inside my gob. 'Look right. Up. Close.' He ticked a box on a clipsheet.

I couldn't believe this. Him ordering me around like a dog.

What was he?

We were in a corridor below the court. Way below. Up there it had been all polished wood and suits saying, *'Terribly sorry. Danger to society. Blah blah blah.'* Down here it were doors with spyholes and peeling paint and the smell of piss.

Fat Face put his clipboard on a table.

'Raise your arms. Stand with your legs apart. This is a rub down search. Part of your daily routine from now on, lad.'

He felt me up all over. *Pervert.*

'Arms down. Take your trainer laces out and remove your belt.'

'Why?' I'd had enough of this.

'To stop you harming yourself. Regulations. Some sensitive young persons in custody find the stress gets to them, see.'

He was trying to freak me out.

'I can handle this.' That belt was cool, bought with my own money.

'Good,' he said, 'but it don't make any difference. Regulations are regulations. Now check this list of what I've taken off you. Phone, keys, belt, laces and £1.96? Right?'

I nodded. Arsehole. He'd had the lot.

'Then sign here. This is your property list. It's going in that red bag. You'll get it back at the end of your sentence. Twelve months, is it?' He looked over my shoulder. 'Oh. L-l-lee Mercer.

Your signature's a bit shaky. You sure you're all right?'

Sarky sod.

I said, 'It's freezing down here.' I were only wearing chinos and a shirt. New. Marks and Sparks. To impress the judge. Waste.

'Ah, the cold.' He nodded. 'Don't feel it myself, not in July. Better put your trainers back on.' He took a key from a bunch on his belt. 'Now let's see what you think of our accommodation, shall we?' He unlocked a door and shoved it open.

'In you go. Go on. In you go.' He smirked. 'Handle it?'

CHAPTER 2

A cell. With tiled walls and a little barred window. High up.

'Go on.' He jangled the keys. 'It's just for a few hours. This is what we call a holding cell. You are now in the custody of the prison service. I've got some ringing round to do to find you a permanent place. Go on. Move.'

A screw then. I felt his mitt on my back. Then the door clanged shut and I heard the key turning in the lock.

A few hours!

I sat on what passed for a bed.

Twelve effing months!

Got up again. Paced the floor. Three steps

one way. Two the other. I've seen dog kennels bigger.

And there was nothing to do.

'I'll always stand by you, Lee.' I could hear Kirstie's words in my head, but she hadn't turned up in court.

Mum was at the front, opposite the dock, looking at her feet or her watch. Wearing her office clothes. She'd smartened up too. And Ken from the community centre, he were at the back, pulling on his beard looking dead sorry.

Hypocrite. He dobbed me in.

And Mum wouldn't look my way. Even when I were sent down. I thought she might say something. Ask the judge for mercy. Or cry.

I were still in cloud-cuckoo-land then.

Twelve effing months! I wanted to shout: *What d'ya mean, arse-face?* But I couldn't. It had got to me. My left knee were shaking. Best not to think about it. Hard not to though. On your own. In the quiet.

Except for the spyhole hatch clattering up and down. About every quarter hour, I reckoned.

It were a relief when all hell broke loose outside the door. Sounded like they were bringing a drunk down. He were effing and blinding and worse. I needed a slash by then and called out, but no one answered.

I should say now, this account would be twice as long if I included all the swearing, so I'll spare you most of it.

Anyway, after a bit I tried sitting on the floor. That way, with my back to the door I could see feet going by the window in the street outside. Normal life carrying on without me. Going to the arcades or the shops or the pub.

In boots with high heels. Trainers with laces. Pink stilettos. Like Kirstie's. *Was it her coming to see me?*

A couple of seagulls swooped down and started fighting over an ice cream on the pavement. Millsford's by the sea but don't get the wrong idea. It's a dump. Talking of which, I thought I might have to add to the brown stains on the floor when I heard the key in the lock. The door opened and a grey-haired granny screw stood there, pointing at a bell by the door.

'If you need the toilet, lad, you press the cell bell.'

Face like a frog. No neck. Could have been a bloke except for the big boobs.

'Come on. It's at the end of the corridor.'

6

She stood watching. Even when I said I needed a dump. And she wouldn't let me flush it away.

'Sorry. We check.' She peered in the bowl. 'Oh dear, is your tummy upset?'

Another pervert.

Later, when I was back in the cell, Fat Face came in with Sonia, my social worker. She was black and decent-looking but useless. Fat Face got her a chair and parked himself by the door.

I sat on the so-called bed.

'You must feel awful, Lee.' She had a face like a wet fortnight.

'Cos you dropped me in it.' She could have got me probation or community service if she'd written a decent report.

'No, Lee. You got yourself in this mess. Sooner you accept that the better.'

'I pinched stuff. Everyone does that.'

'No – they – don't, Lee.' She lowered her posh voice. 'Look, I know it's scary.'

'Not!'

'Then why's your leg shaking?'

'Cos I need a drink!'

'Yes, well. Let's think positively, shall we? You'll get help with that inside – and your temper. A

YOI, a Young Offenders Institution, is a prison, Lee, but it's especially for young people. You'll get counselling and—'

I wondered why the ceiling light had bars over it.

'Counselling?' Fat Face jangled his keys. 'His sort don't learn till someone knocks a bit of sense into them, Miss Benson.'

'Screws had better not touch me. I know my rights.'

'I'm sure you do, lad.' He started to open the door. 'But it's not the prison officers you have to watch out for.'

Sonia got up. 'I will come and see you inside, Lee. It'll be Stoke Heath, I think.' She put her hand in her pocket. 'Oh. Your mum sent this.'

'Cigs! Good old mum, but in't she coming to see me?'

'Sorry, packet's empty. Smoking's not allowed in YOIs. But she's written something on the back.'

No smoking! I couldn't believe it.

Nor Mum not coming to see me.

Nor what she wrote.

CHAPTER 3

Dear Lee,
  Sorry but it won't do my nerves no
good seeing you in there.
  I always said youd end up inside like
your dad and now you have so you just
have to get on with it.
  Mum

Sonia touched my hand. 'You could prove her
wrong, Lee.'

'You read it!'

The uniform stepped between us. 'We have a
right to read your letters, lad. *Now*. And open
your parcels. And listen to your phone calls.'

Sonia said, 'It's for a year, Lee, half that if you keep out of trouble.'

Then they left and the key turned in the lock.

Like your dad.

I were nothing like him.

At some point the granny brought me a slice of pizza, and later on I heard them banging up a few others. But it was the end of the afternoon before the door opened again.

'Right, lad, court's closed now.' Fat Face stood there holding handcuffs. 'Your carriage awaits. Bit of advice before you go, lad. Don't be so lippy. It'll get you in more trouble.'

I'd hardly said a word all day!

But at least we were moving.

'Here, hold out your hands. At the front if you're going to be a good lad.' He cuffed my wrists together. 'Now walk out of the door and wait outside.'

Stop. Wait. Walk forward. Stop. Wait. Walk up the stairs. Wait.

Was this my life from now on?

It were raining in the street outside and there was a white van waiting. Plain, no writing, just a row of little dark windows along the top. A woman yelled 'Scum!' and I wondered if Fat Face would put a blanket over my head like on the news, but he just said, 'Walk to the rear door. Stop. Get into the first sweat box.'

There were six cubicles, like greyhound traps, in the back of the van. With high metal doors. The door of the one just inside was open.

He undid the cuffs. 'Go on. Climb up and sit.'

The engine was running. He closed the door. I pulled down a little seat.

'Got all the files, Rosie?'

'Yup.' It sounded like the granny screw.

I heard her heaving herself in, and the doors shutting. Then I was thrown against the wall as the driver pulled out.

'Don't you know it's against the effing law not to wear effing seat belts?' That was the drunk I think. 'Are you effing listening? I'll see my effing solicitor about this.'

You get the gist? As I said, it's every second word with cons. Some of the others joined in, but the granny didn't answer and after a bit it went quiet, except for the sound of the engine.

I hate quiet.

Like your dad.

I couldn't believe she'd said that.

Did I want to be like my old man? *No.*
Did I want to speak to him? *No.*
Did I want to see him ever again? *No.*
The best thing he did was leave.

After what must have been an hour, the van stopped and someone said Stoke Heath. There was a lot of scraping and beeping and clanging, then the van moved forward. Then it stopped again and I heard doors opening and I stood up. But my door didn't open. The other cons went shuffling past and Granny said, 'You stay there, Lee.'

Funny? *Not.*

It went quiet and I sat down trying not to think.

It's not the screws you have to watch out for.

It was ages before the granny came back and opened my door. She were the same one as before.

'Sorry, Lee, you've got another couple of hours in here. We're going to have to take you to Parkhall. But look on the bright side. It's more modern. Purpose built, so you'll get your own room with a toilet.'

'Oh yeah,' I said. 'And room service?'

She laughed. I'll give her that. 'That's right. You keep your sense of humour.'

Then we were off again and it went quiet once more, except for the engine.

Like your dad. In and out of prison.

Mostly *in*. Strangeways. Life now. He killed someone.

It were better when she started talking.

'Just your mum at home, is there?'

Except that I didn't want to talk about Mum either. Did I want to be like *her*? No, I like to have a laugh sometimes.

'No brothers or sisters?'

'No.'

'It's hard on your own. Has she got a car?'

'No.'

'Oh dear. Parkhall's hard to get to by rail. By the way, if you feel sick on this bendy stretch look out of the window. Above you.' A little square of darkened sky. That's all I could see.

She went on about telephone cards.

I watched the clouds get darker.

She wittered on about health checks.

My neck ached.

She said, 'Motorway soon. Straighter. You'll feel better then.'

But I didn't.

Like your dad.

But I tried to look on the bright side. Parkhall. It didn't sound too bad. Darryl, one of my mates, said YOIs were a piece of . . . well, rhymes with kiss. His mum said it were a holiday camp with TV and everything. I was trying to remember which one he was in, when the van stopped.

'Rush hour,' said Granny. 'We're going to be late. But when you arrive you can ring your mum.'

But will she answer?

You'll have to get on with it.

'If you've got any questions, Lee . . .'

Then the door opened and she was shoving tissues in my hand. As if I were a little kid. Cos I were blubbing like a seven-year-old.

He – my so-called dad – thumped Mum on my birthday. One minute I was opening the present he'd brought me, happy as anything. Scalextric. Next they were screaming at each other and he was throwing cans. Then she was on the floor and he was kicking her head in. And I were crying and trying to pull him off and he slung me from one end of the room to

14

the other. I hit my head against the wall and woke up in casualty. It was one of our many visits to casualty. Mum and me got to know it well. But we stuck together.

Did.

Then.

Granny said, 'Blow. It'll be all right. You can keep the tissues.'

Then she closed the door and the van started moving and I listened to the engine, hoping it would break down so I could make a run for it. Thoughts. How do you stop them when there's nothing else to do? How do you stop your eyes filling up? Or your leg jumping up and down? I felt as if my body had been taken over by aliens.

I tried to think of good stuff like helping this tea leaf on the estate when I was a kid. All I had to do was get in through this little window and open the door for him, so he could get in. Easy peasy. More fun than school and he gave me loads of sweets.

Then the granny said, 'Another ten minutes, Lee. We're going up the driveway leading to Parkhall now. Did I say it's in a park? Used to belong to a stately home.'

Branches crisscrossed the little square window now. Seemed to go on for miles. It was as if we were in a dark forest, and I started to think they were going to dump me in the middle, like those kids in that story with the house made of sweets.

I couldn't believe the thoughts I was having.

Then the van stopped and light streamed through the little square windows. There was a lot of scraping and beeping, like at Stoke Heath, and starting and stopping, then Granny's voice:

'The gates are all double-locked, Lee. We lock the one behind before we open the one in front.'

Then the engine died.

'Stand up, Lee. We're here.' She opened my door, and the rear doors opened at the same time. Two hefty great screws – they had to be, same navy uniform as hers – stood holding the handles.

One said, 'Hello, Rosie. Look at that sunset. Gorgeous, isn't it?'

The other, a baldie, turned to me. 'Get out, lad. I'm . . .'

I think he said his name but I didn't catch it.

I didn't see any sunset either, only huge metal gates slowly closing, and metal walls on either side, topped by coils of razor wire glittering under yellow searchlights.

Holiday camp?

CHAPTER 4

All I wanted to do was get my head down, but the baldie screw had other plans. After the van had been searched – they pushed this little trolley with a mirror on it underneath – he frogmarched me to a brick building that stood separate from another bigger one.

Granny was puffing by the time we reached the door, where Baldie went into the double-locking routine.

'In the room we are about to enter, young persons are searched thoroughly before proceeding to reception and the wing. If you have anything on you that you shouldn't have – weapons or drugs, tobacco or chewing gum – it's best to say so now.'

I said, 'I've been searched already.'

But that made no difference.

It was the same as before – with extras. 'Face me. Look up.' He pushed up my eyelid, then pulled the bottom bit down. I thought he were going to turn me inside out.

Granny ticked the boxes.

'Right, all facial orifices clear. Now bend over.'

I said, 'There's nothing up my arse.'

He said, 'I'll be the judge of that.'

Afterwards he handed me a bottle and told me to go and fill it in the karzy in the corner. I couldn't do it at first, not with him watching. When I did come out, Granny held up a grey tracksuit, three sizes too big.

'You have a choice now, Lee. You can continue to wear your own clothes. Or you can put this on. But I'd advise the tracksuit. You won't look so much like a new boy and you're more likely to see your own clothes again.'

My legs looked like a baby elephant's in the trackie bottoms.

Reception could have been anywhere, school or the health centre on the estate. We had CCTV cameras there. Granny handed over the red bag to a blonde female screw, who emptied all my stuff onto the counter.

'Check if it's all there, lad, and if it is, sign the list at the bottom.' She pointed to a Biro on a chain.

Then the three of them started talking about me as if I weren't there.

'How is he?' The blonde one looked worried. 'We can't do the health check because Health Care have gone home.'

Granny mumbled something and Baldie shook his head. 'Looks perky enough to me. How're you feeling, Lee?'

'OK.' *Not*. I'd have killed for a cig or a Red Bull. Joke.

Baldie leaned over the counter to where they were looking at a computer screen. 'Now, ladies, where are you putting him?'

Granny shook her head. 'No cell free. Seems a couple of lads have smashed theirs up. May's trying to sort something out.'

Cell.

All the nice rooms must have gone.

'Give me the camera then. I'll do another one for the rogues' gallery while we're waiting. Stand over there, Lee, in front of that screen, and hold this board.'

He laughed as I crossed the room. 'Nothing wrong with him. Struts like a bantam cock. Got a good opinion of himself has Lee.'

Good, if that's what he thought.

'Hold up the board, Lee, number facing forward. Don't smile. Look.'

He showed me myself on the little screen. P4340. Like someone on death row.

'Sorted.' The blonde screw handed him a key. 'C-wing, Number 27. You're in luck, Lee. A mate of yours, Darryl, says he's willing to share.'

Darryl! Was my luck turning at last?

Baldie fixed the key to the bunch on his belt. 'Come on.' He unlocked a door. 'Quick march.'

It's not the screws you have to look out for, lad.

But Darryl would show me the ropes. Make sure the others knew I were one of them. Wouldn't let the side down.

'Steady on.' Baldie was locking the door we'd just come through.

I was at the next door looking down a long corridor.

'Not down there. It'd take all night.' He opened a door at the side. 'We're going—'

But the rest of his words were drowned by

21

chanting and yip yipping and loud rhythmic banging.

Afterwards I thought it must be like stepping out of the players' tunnel into a football stadium – if your team were losing and you'd just scored an own goal. I didn't catch all the words. Some I caught but couldn't repeat here. Mostly it were just hooting and jeering. From three tiers of little square windows. With the dark shapes of faces pressed to them.

But I kept my head up. Kept a spring in my step. Kept my arms swinging as I tried to get my bearing.

Don't let them see you're fazed. That would be asking for it. Same as on the estate. *Look confident. Walk tall.* Though I weren't that tall. Not titchy. Average. We were crossing a triangle-shaped yard, buildings on two sides, making a V-shape. Heading for a door in the middle.

The screw said, 'C-wing. B spur's the one on the right.'

Inside, the noise throbbed right through you.

'Pipe-banging,' said the screw, closing the door we'd come through. 'You'll get used to it.' He opened another door. 'Upstairs, right to the top.'

The metal stairs vibrated under my feet and

by the time I got to the top I were sweating. I were dead keen to see Darryl.

Then he opened a door.

What had the old bat said? Modern? Purpose-built? Well, think of all the prison films you've seen. Think long lines of metal doors with spy hatches. Think landings on four sides of a rectangle. The only modern bit was the mesh strung between them.

'Safety,' the screw said. 'We're very hot on safety. We do try to take care of our young persons.' He pointed to the space below. 'That's the Association Area where you meet up for an hour a day. Walk on.'

What did they do for the rest of the time?

Number 27 was near the end of the line, in the corner. When we reached it, Baldie stood with the key in his hand.

'This cell is temporary, Lee. You will have your own soon. That's the policy at Parkhall. We think single occupancy is best, but over-crowding sometimes makes that difficult.'

Get on with it. Open up. I don't mind sharing. Darryl's my mate.

'Two more things. Firstly my name is Mr Sampson and from now on you'll use my name

when you speak to me. Not Slaphead or Baldie
or anything else—'

'I never.'

'No, but you probably thought it, and what
you think, you tend to say.'

Don't know why he was so touchy about it.
It's the fashion. Mine's shaved really close. Mind
you, I ain't got fuzz halfway round my face.

'So I'll think of you as a young person,' he
went on. 'Not prisoner, inmate, con or yob or
any other rude word, and I will call you Lee.
You will think of me as an officer, not screw,
guard or warder, and you will call me Mr
Sampson. Some officers allow "guy" or "boss".
That's up to them. The idea is you show respect
to us. We show respect to you. That's how it
works in here. Right? Right, Lee?'

'Right.' Anything to get rid of him.

'Right?' He tapped the floor with his heavy
black boot.

'Right, Mr Sampson.' *Arsehole.*

'That's better.' He slid back the hatch.

'OK, Darren, I'm coming in with your cell
mate now.'

Darren? I said, 'Hold on a sec.'

But the door was open and I could see inside.

'Hello, Leesie.'

Someone sat hunched in the shadows on the top bunk.

Leesie? I hadn't been called that since way back, and it gave me bad vibes.

CHAPTER 5

Not my mate.

When he slithered down from the bunk into the light from the door, I sort of recognized him. But that didn't make me feel better. A ferret. That's what he reminded me of. Long, thin and slippery.

Darren? I racked my brains.

He had close-together eyes and a little black fringe.

'We went to school together, we did, Mr Sampson. Lived on the same estate.'

The screw said, 'Are you all right with this?'

Darren Jackson. But they called him Sharpey. It came to me. He used to play around with knives. Was that what he was in for? He lived in the other high-rise on the Churchill estate. Ages ago.

What would the screw do if I said 'No'? How would it play?

But I nodded. Better the devil you know.

Though I didn't know.

'Was that a yes, Lee? Then say, "Yes, Mr Sampson" and I'll leave you two to catch up.'

'It's best to play by the rules, Leesie.' Sharpey sounded as if butter wouldn't melt. 'Speak up and take your hands out of your pockets.'

He had to be taking the piss.

The screw said, 'That's right, Darren, put Lee on the right track. Tell him how the system works. Ah, here's Mr Armstrong with your first night pack, Lee.'

A black screw with a beard handed me a plastic bag. Then they both went out and I heard the key turn in the lock.

'Jimjams,' said Sharpey, 'and a toothbrush and a writing pad so you can write to your mum. And a telephone card. That's useful. You can ring her tonight. How is she?'

He'd climbed back onto the top bunk and turned up the TV, which was fixed to the wall behind the door. *Who Wants to be a Millionaire?* But all I could hear was the pipe-banging.

Sharpey? A picture of him came into my mind, hazy. Chubby. Not like now. On the edge of the playground. He was right; we had been to the same school. When we were little kids. When we went.

'Sit down.' He pointed to the lower bunk where there was a pile of bedding wrapped in plastic. 'That's yours. I get first dibs. You have to make it up yourself. They brought the bunks in when I said I didn't mind sharing. Not with you, Leesie. You're OK, you are. Homey, isn't it?'

It was about three metres by two metres and what you might call customized. Not bare like the holding cell. The walls were covered with girlie photos cut out of mags and newspapers and there was a curtain over the barred window. He'd even made a little holder for his toothbrush out of a Colgate packet. It was Sellotaped to the wall above the sink.

'*En suite.*' He pointed to the karzy behind the door. 'Stainless steel.'

But it weren't – stainless, I mean. Sharpey must just have had a dump from the look of it. There weren't no lid.

He said, 'You can clean it if you like. There's the brush.' There were bottles of cleaning stuff too, lots of them in the corner under the sink, and a dustpan and brush.

He made a show of looking at his watch.

'Half past eight. Got this from the Argos catalogue – and the curtains. I'm a good boy, see, so I'm on Enhanced. I get privileges. You'll start on Standard, but you can work yourself up to Enhanced – or down to Basic if you're naughty. That's how it works – rewards and punishments.'

He laughed as if I'd looked scared. 'Nothing you can't handle, Leesie. It'll make a man of you. Now, did they give you the rule book?'

They hadn't.

'I'll have to help you then. Had anything to eat?'

I shook my head.

'Press the bell then.'

It was by the door. I pressed and nothing happened so I opened the pack. Pyjamas: grey, toothbrush: grey – and the telephone card.

Who would I ring?

I thought about it while I made up the bed with the sheets and blanket. Grey.

Kirstie? Mum? Pizza Hut?

The pipe-banging was doing my head in. So was thinking about Kirstie. The Page 3 girls on the walls didn't help. Mr Nobby jumped to attention.

Was she doing it with someone else already?

Then Sharpey's ferret face was hanging over the side like one of those ugly heads on a church wall.

'Leesie, I just said, "Here's Mr Armstrong".'

Don't know how he heard.

A deep voice outside the door said, 'What is it? What do you want?'

'New boy here hasn't had anything to eat, guv. Or his phone call. You could get in trouble for that. Human rights.'

Later, the black, bearded screw tossed in a packet of sandwiches and something else in Cellophane.

'Corn fakes,' said Sharpey. 'You'll see what I mean. For breakfast tomorrow – and milk. Powdered, I'm afraid, and tea and coffee. You can make a cup now if you like.'

There was a kettle on the floor beside my bunk, but my appetite had gone.

I said, 'You seem to be well in with the screws, Sharpey.'

'I'm well in with everyone. You've got to be in here. That's why you need your phone call. Get visitors to bring stuff in. Currency, see. To pay your taxes. *Trade with.* I'll explain. Be careful how you put it, mind. They record the calls. Ask for shampoo and snacks for starters. Consumables don't go on your property list so they don't get checked.'

He said hard property like watches and iPods went on a list which was checked against what you had whenever the screw felt like it.

'To guard against thieving and bullying and nasty stuff like that. Some of the cons aren't very nice, Leesie.'

I tried to ring Kirstie later when the screw took me down to the phones. They were on the wall in the open space below the landings, where there were tables for pool and table tennis. If the screw was listening he must have been disappointed. Kirstie weren't there. Or she weren't answering. Nor was Mum.

I'll always stand by you, Lee.

Yes, well. Sod it. My eyes started stinging.

I saw the screw look the other way.

But back in the cell, Sharpey didn't. 'Oh dear.

Out on the town, were they? Well, if you haven't got currency, you'd better make sure you can take care of yourself. I'm armed. See.' He picked up his toothbrush from its little holder and made with it as if it were a little sword.

I laughed.

Till I saw the razor blade hidden in the bristles.

The cell light went out at ten, but I couldn't get to sleep. There was too much going on in my head, despite the noise. I asked Sharpey what time it all stopped and he said never. Some of the window warriors went on all night pipe-banging and shouting at each other.

The light outside filled the cell with a yellowy glow. I didn't mind that. It was better than the dark.

'Another tip, Leesie.' Sharpey was awake too. 'Don't let no one know what you're in for.'

How did he know what I was in for?

'It wouldn't go down well.'

I said, 'I can handle this. OK?'

But to tell the truth, I weren't so sure no more.

CHAPTER 6

Somehow I got to sleep and woke to the sound of running water. Mum in the shower, I thought, till I opened my eyes.

'Morning, Leesie.'

Sharpey was in the corner near the karzy. I thought he was doing the obvious till I saw a plastic bowl in his hand.

'Tasty.'

'You got a better way?' He was holding his cornflakes under the tap.

'Mixing the milk powder with water first?'

'Please yourself.'

I did, later, but they still tasted like soggy cardboard.

'Corn fakes,' he said. 'Told you, and don't let the kettle come to the boil, or the cup'll melt. Safety. Some cons kept *slipping* with cups of boiling water and sugar in their hands. We get some nasty accidents inside, Leesie.'

He climbed up to the top bunk with his tea. I watched the granules float in my coffee as a couple of suits on breakfast TV ummed and ahed about the rising crime rate.

'And you'd better get out of those jimjams quick, Leesie. You've got an exciting day ahead. Induction. That's when the screws tell you how to keep on their right side. But you listen to me – there's just one golden rule inside, Leesie. Don't grass.'

I knew that.

'Second rule? Know who to look out for and pay your taxes. There's Errol. He's black, well, so are half the cons, but he's the biggest. He'll want your phone card for dealing. And there's Craig. Well, you'll soon spot Craig. They're both from Camden but rival gangs and the screws haven't caught onto that yet. They've just moved Craig from D-wing to split him up from his gang. He'll be looking for recruits. No, you can't have one.'

He'd seen me watching him scoff biscuits.

'I bought these with my earnings. For going to classes. Education is a wonderful thing, Leesie. And if you don't do it you're banged up all day.'

Then the door opened and a screw with a shaved head and an earring said he'd be back at 8.30 to take me to the health centre.

Sharpey shook his head. 'Weren't you checked over last night then? Deary me, this place is going to pot in more ways than one.'

I asked what they did in the health check.

'Take the piss. And blood. And other bodily fluids. To see if you're a dope head or a junkie or HIV or about to top yourself. Don't worry about it. You get a nice walk through the park.'

Park. That did make me laugh.

But he weren't having me on.

I couldn't believe it when the screw, Mr Williams, opened the second gate in the outer fence. It were like stepping through a magic door. Abracadabra. Grey turned to green and red and yellow. A park. Not like for kids with swings and roundabouts, but grass and trees and flowers and birds hopping about.

'Don't get the wrong idea.' The screw was locking the gate behind us. 'You can't see the perimeter fence but it's there and it's touch sensitive. And there's CCTV.' He pointed to a white building that you could just see through the trees. 'There's the health centre. Go on. Follow the yellow brick road.'

It was a gravel path and there were cons weeding it, wearing red bibs over their grey tracksuits. We had to step round them. More cons were working on the flowerbeds at the side. Mr Williams nodded at the screw supervizing them, but didn't stop to talk.

'Gardening's popular, Lee. A lot of lads work towards a qualification, so they can work in parks and gardens when they get out. Obviously you have to prove yourself trustworthy before you're allowed out here.'

One con was driving a ride-on mower. Cool, except that it reminded me of Mrs Brown. Not that she'd had a ride-on.

Mrs Brown, the reason I were in here.

How did Sharpey know about her?

★

'Right, Lee. C'mere.' Sister Rogers, the nurse in charge of the health centre was Irish, I think. Or Scottish.

'Now get yourself in that cubicle and strip off. Then put on the dressing gown and come out here.'

At least she didn't do screw-speak. It weren't 'young person this' and 'young person that'. She didn't look like a screw either. Another granny – don't think they allowed young females inside – her face was dead wrinkly, but her top were bright pink and so were her hair.

'I get fed up with grey, don't you? Em . . .' she took hold of my chin. 'You feeling a bit queasy?'

'It's the smell.'

Took me back a bit.

'But better than on the wing, is it not? '

She could say that again. Think boiled cabbage and sweaty trainers.

'Right, roll up your right sleeve. Let us find a vein. Grand.' She had a bloody great needle in her hand, and by the end of the morning she'd taken so many samples of my bodily fluids I felt drained.

I said, 'What do you do with it all?'

She laughed. 'Don't touch the soup.' Then she started firing questions at me, from a clipboard. How many times a week did I eat red meat? How much fruit? How many times a week did I exercise? How many units of alcohol a week?

How the hell did I know?

'We're trying to get a picture of your lifestyle outside,' she said. 'To see what changes you need to make. You can turn yourself round in here, Lee, if you stick to the rules. Halve your sentence, you can. And, think about this, *you need never come back here.*'

When I got back to the cell, at about four o'clock, Sharpey sat sniggering on the top bunk. 'Did you get the Safe Sex talk?'

I did, but still couldn't believe it. That wrinkly talking about condoms. And not just talking. There were two more new boys by then, and she'd sat the three of us – Harley, Wayne and me – in front of a flip chart with diagrams and everything. Everything. No detail spared. And she'd gone on and on about HIV and AIDS and safe sex.

Harley, who looked about seven, didn't say

anything. He'd been blubbing in the next cubicle at one point. I'd heard the nurse say, 'Cheer up, lad. If you can't do the time, don't do the crime. That's what I say. Your dad called David, is he?'

He'd said, 'How do you know, miss?' in this posh voice.

She said, 'A lot of men want a motorbike and get a baby.'

But he didn't say nothing after that. Nor did I.

Luckily the one called Wayne – he had tattoos all over his head – said what I'd been thinking.

'I don't get it. What's the point of this? Are there girls here?'

And she'd said, 'Dream on, love. I'm giving you good advice for when you get outside. But think about it. You are in here for a long time and may find yourself doing things you would never have dreamed of doing outside.' Then she'd blown up a Johnny like a balloon.

Did she really mean what I thought she meant?

'You don't have to,' she went on, 'and in my

book it's best not to, but if you do, use one of these.'

Wayne exploded. 'I'm not effing gay!'

She said, 'No, you probably aren't. Gays in my experience tend to be gentle, polite sort of people, but some lads in here are not. So watch your back, especially in the showers.'

I still couldn't believe it.

Sharpey said, 'We all cope in different ways. You'd be surprised. But don't worry about it. Here catch this.'

A spliff.

I threw it back up. 'I don't.'

I'm not saying I've never, but if getting out sooner meant going without, I'd go without. I could still hear the nurse saying six months instead of twelve.

He said, 'Everyone needs a little help from time to time, Leesie.'

He reached down to give it me again, and I saw the scars on his arm, one still bleeding. So that's what he used his little blade for.

'No thanks, Sharpey.' If he'd offered Red Stripe it might have been different.

He said, 'Please yourself, but that spliff was a

present from a friend and it don't do to offend friends in here.'

I said, 'I need a kip.' I did and I'd had more than enough of being told what to do by Sharpey and everyone else.

But I should have stayed awake.

CHAPTER 7

A white-haired screw was shaking my arm.

'Stand by your bed.'

Random check. A rub down search.

He found the spliff in my pocket.

'Where did you get this?'

'Dunno.' But I did.

Sharpey was already on the floor standing to attention. The screw made a note in a book, and pocketed the spliff.

'You'll be hearing more about this. I'm charging you with being in possession of an unauthorized article, which will be tested to establish its contents.'

Sharpey was a model prisoner. 'Sorry, Mr

O'Hara, I haven't explained all the rules to Lee yet. Come on, Leesie. Hotplate now. This is when we get our tea and you'll meet the neighbours.'

We had to wait on the landing while the screw locked the door behind us.

I said, 'I'll get you for this, Sharpey.'

He pretended he hadn't heard.

'Hotplate's down in Sosh, Leesie. Association Area.' He pointed to the space below where the games tables and the phones were.

I were seething inside. He'd dropped me in it. But a big black con with rasta hair, just out of the cell next door, gripped my hand.

'This your new little friend, Sharpey?' He held onto my hand.

Sharpey said, 'Meet Leesie, Errol.'

I said, 'Lee. It's Lee.'

'How'ya doing, Lee?' Voice like a chainsaw, the black con pumped my hand up and down.

But as we went along the landing, with the screws letting other cons out, he jumped about, shadow-boxing someone only he could see.

'Just do what I do,' said Sharpey when we got to the bottom of the stairs. He led the way to the side of the area where there was a queue leading to a long table. At the top of it a female screw stood marking a clipboard.

Sharpey picked up a tray and a plastic knife and fork and I did the same. I was starving. I'd only had sandwiches at dinner time.

'Nice haircut, innit?' Errol, just behind me, patted the top of my head. 'You look like a real con, man.'

The white-haired screw took a step towards him.

'Evening, guv. Chatting to the new boy. Make him feel at home, like.'

The screw stayed close.

'I was about to ask him if Sharpey has explained all the rules. It's important to obey the rules, isn't it, guv?'

The screw gave him a leery look and Sharpey, just in front, shuffled forward.

'It's bangers, chips and beans or bangers, chips and beans tonight, Leesie.'

Another con, cropped hair stiff with gel, was on his way back, head down, guarding his plate with his arm.

'Gi' us a chip, Craig.' Errol reached out.

'Get lost, black guy.' Craig. He looked up and I saw why Sharpey said I'd spot him easily. He had a scar from the middle of his forehead to halfway down his cheek, right through his left eye. Or the puckered bit of skin where his left eye used to be.

'That's racist, Craig man. You hear that, guv? This con disrespecting me.'

But the screw had moved on to talk to the female with the clipboard.

I tried not to look at Craig, but he were still standing there, and his non-eye were repulsive and magnetic at the same time. Then I caught a whiff of the grub already plated up on the hotplate. Couldn't be hot, not on plastic plates, but it looked like it would do the business. A con on the other side of the table was dishing up.

Sharpey said, 'That's one of the best jobs, that is, but you've got to be well in with the officers to get that. Go on. Take a plate. And pick up a pack. Tomorrow's breakfast.'

Officers? Yeah, the white-haired screw was in hearing distance.

There was a pile of packets of cornflakes and milk just before you got to the hotplate. I was about to pick one up, when a spike-haired con with a scabby mouth mumbled something at me.

When I didn't answer he gripped my arm. 'I said, what you got?'

'Nothing yet.' I thought he meant grub.

'I mean,' he edged closer, 'what you bring in, like? Cigs? Skunk? Works?'

I glanced round, but the screw had moved away. Was gabbing to another with a ponytail.

'They searched me, man.'

I picked up a plate. Bangers, chips and beans.

'The full jobby, was it?' Scab Face laughed. 'Well, just remember to pay your dues.'

'With glue?' You could smell it on his breath. 'Sorry, man, I forgot to stick a tube up my arse.'

'Comedian yeah?' He leaned over. 'Well, watch this, funny man.'

He grabbed one of my bangers. Well, I weren't letting him get away with that. Straight back, I went for one of his, would have got it if One-eye hadn't come back and kneed me in the nuts.

'Quiet if you don't want a repeat.' Calm as anything, One-eye took my other banger. 'I'll leave Sharpey to explain.'

Doubled up, I saw the sod heading for the door to the stairs, where the white-haired screw was unlocking it with his back to me. Had he seen what One-eye'd done? Had the others? If they had, they weren't saying.

'Move along now.' The ponytailed screw was at the front of the queue with the clipboard. 'If you've got your plate go back to your cell. Go on, all of you.'

He didn't seem to notice mine was half empty or that I was in agony.

'It's like this,' said Sharpey when we were back in the cell. 'You've got to play the game. Games. There are several. There's the screws' games and there's the cons' games. You shouldn't have upset Scab Face because he works for Craig. So Craig moved in to protect him.'

I needed to remember who everyone was.

Scab Face was the glue-head. Craig was the one-eyed thug with the scar. I wouldn't forget him.

'I made a joke.'

'Well, he didn't see it. You handled that badly.' He climbed up to the top bunk. 'Another thing, you made a mistake with Errol too. He sent you the spliff. You should have said thank you.'

'You planted that.'

'I was only trying to help you, Leesie. Bit of bad luck the screw deciding to check you out.'

I didn't say anything. My nuts were still hurting.

'It's about respect. You've got to earn it. See, some of the guys in here, they've done serious stuff. I do mean serious. So at the moment you're like lowest of the low. Not as low as the nonces. Not Of Normal Criminal Element.' He shook his head. 'Oh, Leesie, you've got such a lot to learn. Trouble is, you're not bright and you're not hard. No one's scared of you, Leesie. By the way, Mick sends his regards.'

Mick? Who was he talking about?

'Mick Donaghue. He told me to look after you.'

Mick Donaghue. Alarm bells rang in my head as some of the haze cleared. He was the loan shark on the estate and a fence, and yes − that was it − Sharpey did 'errands' for him. If someone got behind with their payments, Mick sent Sharpey round to tell them to pay up. Before he sent in the heavy mob. My mum had borrowed from Mick, and that was another part of why I were in here...

But best not to go there. Anyway, Sharpey had lost no time in letting him know I were in here, and Mick knew I could drop him in it. So he'd told Sharpey to keep an eye on me. Make sure I kept quiet.

I said, 'Drop one, Sharpey. You don't know nothing.'

Trouble was, he knew far too much.

CHAPTER 8

My nuts still hurt next morning.

The screw with the earring, Mr Williams, turned up after breakfast. Not the chatty type, he didn't even say where we were going. I hoped it were to the park, but when we got outside he started crossing the yard. And the pipe bangers struck up.

'New con Lee,
New con Lee,
Had his nuts squeezed
In Wing C.'

The screw didn't seem to hear it, and I had this crazy thought that he was going to tell me it was all a mistake and I was going home. He were heading back to Reception, but when we got inside, he turned right into a different part.

'The education block, to meet your personal officer.'

There were classrooms either side of a long corridor, but he took me to the door at the end. It said MR McGIVEN on the door.

The screw knocked.

'Enterrrrr!'

This ginger screw, moustache like a cat's tail, sat behind a desk straightening a wad of papers.

'Lee Merrrrrrcer?' He stood up and shook my hand. 'Yes? Sit down, Lee.'

To say he was Scottish and proud of it, was well, true. He even had a photo of himself, well I thought it were him, in a kilt, standing by a bird in a long dress. It were on a shelf behind him.

'Rrrrright, let's get starrrrted. Firrrst, I'll apologize for things being a bit topsy-turrrrvy since your arrival.'

Topsy-turvy! Who *was* this?

Now, you know what I said about all the effing and blinding, that this would be twice as long if I put it all in? Well the same goes for his arrrrrring.

'Now, Lee, I'm your personal officer for the duration of your stay. I am a prison officer, as you can see from the uniform, but I'll be working closely with your YOT – Youth Offender Team – but I'm sure you know that. Anyway, Lee, Personal Officer means you come to me if you have any worries in here. Right?'

There was another photo of a bloke in army uniform holding a bayonet. Him? The one in the photo had more hair, on top of his head that is.

'Yes, that's me. But look at me, lad, when I'm speaking to you, and have the manners to respond. Have you got any worries?'

How long have you got?

'If you've experienced any abuse or bullying so far, tell me now and I'll see the perpetrators are dealt with. Ah, I see you're sharing a cell. How's that going?'

'I'd rather be on my own.' That seemed safe enough.

'Yes, well, we'll get that sorted as soon as possible. Your welfare is of paramount importance to me. Pa-rrrrrr-amount. But' – he leaned forward and fixed me with a stare – 'staff need to know if there are rackets inside. We can't help if we don't know.'

So why don't they open their eyes?

'I want to make one thing clear. You have a choice, Lee, to come out of here a better person or – well, let's think positively, shall we?' He squared up the paper in front of him. 'Now I'd like you to look at this.'

It was a questionnaire headed: What Do You Think?

'Can you read?'

'Yes.'

'Good. Half the lads here can't and we help with that. We will assess your reading ability later. Now, the purpose of this questionnaire is to identify the reasons why you offend. Yes?'

I nodded.

'And reduce these factors. Yes? So you don't offend again.'

Easy peasy. All very logical. He hadn't a clue. I yawned. Couldn't help it.

He stroked his droopy moustache. 'How'd you sleep last night, Lee?'

'I didn't.' Well, not till the early hours.

'Any particular reason?'

I kept quiet and he found a note in my file. 'Oh.' His face fell. 'I see you're on a charge already. For possession of a spliff.'

Because Sharpey planted one on me.

'Where did you get it?'

I kept quiet.

'A bad start.' He wrote something down. 'You were searched when you came inside. You didn't bring it in. So where did you get it? It will go better for you if you say.'

Don't grass.

'OK, but think about it before you go before the governor, right? As I said, you've got to make a choice. Back to the form. First question. About your family and where you live. Let's look at this statement. *Some young people stay away from home without asking.* Were you a) just like that b) quite like that c) a bit like that or d) not like that at all?'

I said, 'A bit like that.' Because mostly I went home at night. Nowhere else to go.

'Right. Second statement. *Some young people know that members of their family care about them.* Would you say you're a) just like that b) quite like that c) a bit like that or d) not like that at all?'

You'll have to get on as best you can.

'Dunno.'

'That's a cop out. If you say "dunno" you've got to say why you don't know.'

I shrugged.

He shuffled papers. 'I see there's just you and your mum at home. What does she do for you? Cooking? Ironing?'

'Sometimes.'

'Isn't that caring?'

I settled for 'c' but I didn't really know. Didn't know the answer to most of them and there were *fifty*. And when we got to the end of them, he handed me another wad of paper.

He laughed. 'Don't worry. This is for you to fill in later when you have a release date, but you can read it in your spare time. It's about all the training courses you can do here, to improve your chances of finding a job. If you have a job you have money and don't need to steal. That's the idea.' He looked me in the eye. 'Would you say that's what you stole for? Money? To buy stuff?'

'I just do it.'

'Well, you need to think why. How do you feel when you're doing a job?'

'Feel?' What had that got to do with it?

'Is it exciting? Give you a buzz?'

I thought about all that climbing in windows. 'Yeah. When I were a kid it were exciting.'

'And what about when you mugged the old

lady? Mrs Brown.' He had read my notes. 'Resulting in ABH. Was *that* exciting?'

'Sort of, but I didn't mean to hurt her. It were a spur of the moment thing.'

'Go on.'

'Me and my mates were on the seafront. Hanging about. Fancied a bevvy but none of us had any dosh. Then we saw this old lady tottering out of the post office, and one of them said, "Dare you to get her bag. Bet she's just got her pension." And I was off. Charging across the road. For a laugh, but when I made a grab for her bag, she started hitting me with her stick. And she didn't let go. And I could hear the others laughing and jeering. "Couldn't take sweets off a baby!" That sort of thing, and she hung on to her bag and we struggled a bit and she tripped.'

He was looking at me. Waiting. I felt pinned to the wall.

'Well, I may have pushed her. When I lost my rag. When the others were having a go.'

He raised a bushy eyebrow.

'But I didn't hit her.'

'And all this came about because you were bored and hadn't any money? And no job to earn any? And because you, er, "lost your rag"?'

I nodded.

'Well, Lee, while you're here let's see if you can find something here to stave off the boredom and earn you some money.' He pointed to the list. 'Read the list while I make a phone call.'

Painting and Decorating. Industrial cleaning. No thanks.

Engineering. Child care. Definitely not. *Gardening.* That would get me outside. *ITC. Drama. Radio, Film and Video.* Quite fancy being a disc jockey. *Gym.* Or a personal trainer? *Construction? Motor vehicles?* I asked if that were learning to drive, but he said it was maintaining and repairing vehicles.

'But it might help you get a job with cars. We aim to give you skills you can use outside, see. But you've got to do your bit first, like catching up on some of the basic schooling you've missed and learning to control your temper. You'll need classes in Anger Management and oh . . .' That look again. 'Not so good. I see you've got another case coming up. Burglary. That could double your sentence.'

Double it!

'But let's be positive. That's all the more

reason to do well here. If we can say you're co-operating fully, the judge might take that into consideration.'

'Yes, guv.' *The sooner I got out the better.* I'd decided.

'So, take your time to get used to this place. Keep your head down and don't go looking for trouble.'

Look for it!

'Yes – guv.'

But I was dying for a slash and had to ask. Like in the infants. He looked at his watch.

'It's time we finished anyway. Take that list of training courses with you and think about it. Talk it over with some of the others.'

He stood up. 'Now, remember, if you have a problem, ask to speak to me. Each morning after breakfast an officer will ask if you have any special requests. It might be for the canteen or a Visiting Order. If you want someone to visit you, you have to fill in a form with their name and address. Ah, here's Mrs Beddoes to take you back to the wing. This afternoon you'll return to Education to do more assessment tests.'

The short-haired blonde screw, who'd been in Reception on my first night, was standing in the doorway.

Mr McGiven said, 'Lee needs the toilet. Take him to the one at the end of the corridor, will you? Then take him back to C-wing.'

By the time we'd been through the locking and unlocking routine I was bursting. To make it worse, the screw never shut up about the Scottish screw. I think she had the hots for him.

'You're very lucky getting Mr McGiven. Firm but fair, he is. Was in the Black Watch in Iraq. Do as he says, think positive and you'll be all right.'

But I couldn't think anything, hopping from one leg to another.

Shut up and open the door.

There were three cubicles. No doors or seats but at least the screw didn't come in with me.

So she didn't see who was behind the door.

CHAPTER 9

I didn't see him at first.

I went straight for a slash in the first cubicle. It was when I turned round that I saw the big black con with the rasta hair. He had his finger over his lips.

If I hadn't just been, I'd have wet myself.

Mrs Beddoes called out, 'You all right in there, lad?' The door was still half open.

Errol, that was his name, mimed going for a dump. I couldn't help laughing, but he jerked his head towards the door.

Catching on, I said, 'Just going for a dump, Mrs Beddoes!'

I don't know if she heard, because her radio

beeped and she started talking to someone — and the door snapped shut — and Errol's hand was in front of me, like a big, pink starfish.

'Phone card, man.'

'**** ***!'

But his hand was round my throat before I could get the words out. I jerked up my knee but he moved so fast, I was back against the karzy, before I could reach his nuts.

'Dance like a butterfly. Sting like a bee, man. You owes me, yeah.'

The door was still closed.

'I know you got one, man, and there's credit on it, innit? I know you didn't get through to your old lady last night. Or your little girlfriend. I sorry about that, man, but every cloud got a silver, innit? So move it, man, before I breaks your neck.'

'If — you — could — let — go.'

I couldn't see what I was doing with his hands round my neck.

He giggled. 'You's a fighter, man. I like you, yeah?' But he didn't loosen his grip.

I turned my pockets inside out and the card fell to the floor.

'Pick it up, man.'

I expected his boot in my face, but he was all smiles.

'Yeah, well good, man, but you shouldn't drop litter, innit?'

The list of training courses was on the floor. I picked it up, taking my time. Trying to think and look out for myself.

He laughed. 'You need to get down the gym, boy. That's all the training you need. You's a fighter but you need more muscle. Anyhow, you learned something today. You help Errol. Errol help you.'

I put the list in my pocket. He put my phone card in his.

It had gone quiet outside. The screws had stopped talking on their radios. He pushed me back in the cubicle and mimed pulling the chain, though there was a handle not a chain. I flushed the karzy and as I came out, the door opened. Mrs Beddoes stuck her head in and saw us both.

'Ah, Errol, is that you in there? I thought I heard voices.'

'Mrs Beddoes! Hold on a minute!' Errol made a show of checking in the sheet of Perspex that passed for a mirror.

'Yes! YES!' He giggled. 'It's still me-e, innit? I'm still here, Mrs B!'

I saw him later phoning during Association. Sosh. That was the hour after hotplate when we were allowed out of our cells to mix. Some of us, depending how many screws were on duty. Tonight there were three screws watching about a dozen of us.

I was at the pool table watching Sharpey play against Craig, One-eye, who seemed to be potting for most of the time. Scab Face, his sidekick, had taken a break from being his parrot. He was playing table football with the new boy, Wayne, the one with the tattooed head. Tattoo-head seemed to be getting on OK.

Harley, the other new one, still looked as if he was going to burst into tears. He was waiting for a turn at the phone, card in hand. How come he'd managed to hang onto his and I hadn't? The white-haired screw, was standing beside him. Looked like a bodyguard. But how long could that last? I didn't fancy the posh kid's chances. You had to be able to look after yourself in this place. Like on the estate. There weren't many who got one over me there. So why were they managing it here?

Because you couldn't lie low? Because trouble came looking for you?

I were going to have to find a way to protect myself.

Sharpey said, 'Aren't you gonna phone your mum?'

The female screw who had been on hotplate duty last night was standing right by. Talking to a baby-faced con.

'Nah.' I hadn't told him about Errol and the card.

'You should do, Leesie. As I said, you need to tell her about visiting.' He raised his voice. 'It's nice having visitors, isn't it, Mrs James? Keeping in touch with friends and family. It's important. Makes you less likely to re-offend, Leesie. '

We both watched Errol put down the phone and shove my card in his pocket. Then he had a word with two other black cons who were doing sudoku together.

The baby-faced con said, 'Errol was phoning his dad, I think.'

'Thought his card had run out,' said an Asian con.

And Sharpey looked at me. He didn't say anything, but he knew. I could see it on his face. I swear his nose twitched.

When the screw moved away he said, 'I hope you've got something for Craig as well.'

'Why?'

''Cos when he finds out about Errol he won't be happy.'

'How will he find out?'

'He'll think you've joined Errol's gang.'

'What if I have?' It started to seem like a good idea. Strength in numbers. If you can't beat them ... If the one-eyed con and Scab Face were against me, wouldn't it be best to have the big guy on my side?

'Please yourself, but I think it's best to keep everyone sweet. Tell you what, I'll tell Craig you're on the case.'

Before I could say 'don't bother', he sidled back to the pool table where he wasn't getting much of a game.

I went and sat at the side, on a bench fixed to the wall. The baby-faced con came up and sat down beside me. Close.

I said, 'Have you paid for two seats?'

He said, 'No. You don't have to pay for them.

They're free. What's your opinion of digitalization?'

There was a laugh from someone. 'You tell him all about it, Stumpy!'

Stumpy. It suited him. He had a big round head with baby hair like velvet, and his belly hung over his waistband.

I moved away a bit and Errol came and sat on my other side and slipped something into my pocket.

'Tell him all about it, Stumpy, and don't forget the analogues.'

Everyone laughed – except the one they were laughing at – and Errol wandered off.

'Do you think it's a good thing or a bad thing?' Stumpy went on. And on.

I didn't answer but it made no difference. He kept going in this dead serious voice about analogues and TV and stuff. Definitely a sandwich short of a picnic, but sort of clever with it.

Weird.

Craig punched the air silently as he won his game against Sharpey, who stayed talking to him. I guessed what about and expected One-eye to come over. But he went to join Scab

Face, who was still playing Wayne at table football.

Trying to throw off Stumpy, I went over to
the pool table, but Errol and another guy beat
me to it, and Stumpy stuck.

'Digitalization is a big step in my opinion.'

The screws seemed more watchful that night.
Well, Mr McGiven was. It was the first time I'd
seen him on the wing, and his eyes were all over
the place, as if he were looking out for land-
mines and snipers. I thought that might have
been why Craig didn't come over, or even look
in my direction. But I learned later that weren't
his style.

When we were lining up to go back to the
cells, I smelled Scab Face behind me.

'Craig says you gave the black fella your phone
card.'

Craig says.

'So?' I hated them two. My nuts still hurt.

I felt him finger my collar. 'Nasty marks you
got there. Craig says you should give your stuff
to someone more appreciative.'

'Craig says.' I flapped my arms and
squawked.

And Mr McGiven came over. 'Keep your

distance, you two. Both of you take one step back.'

He stayed to see his order carried out, but soon after that he got a message on his radio and left. I heard him ask the other two if they could do the banging up. I suppose they felt safe enough with their radios and CCTV cameras all over the place.

There was one on the landing outside our cells. In the ceiling covering the doors. It was when Mr O'Hara, the white-haired guy, was letting Errol into his cell that Scab Face got close enough to deliver another 'Craig says'.

His cell was further up the landing. Not that he needed to be quiet with all the clanging and banging. Also Errol never stopped talking and the female screw, Mrs Beddoes, was jabbering away to Harley, who'd been put in the cell on the other side of ours.

Anyway, I was wondering how the screws had managed to find separate cells for Wayne and Harley who had come in after me, when I smelled glue and Scab Face nudged me.

'Craig says . . . '

I yawned.

He smirked, cracking a scab near his gob.

'Have it your own way. But you should be more grateful — if you care about personal safety.'

Was I scared?

Do dogs poo on pavements?

But I shrugged.

CHAPTER 10

Ferret features was full of advice.

'Thing is, Leesie, you haven't got any stuff to keep the other cons happy and you need some. Order some from the canteen.'

Canteen equalled shop, but not a proper shop. You just got a list of stock once a week, and you ticked what you wanted. Then the screws brought it to the cell. OK if you had money. But I hadn't.

'You'd better write to your mum, Leesie. And get a Visiting Order for her.'

I remembered her so-called letter.

'And your bird if you've got one.'

Had I got one?

'If you want to keep in with Big Craig.'

'*Big?* He's a short arse.'

'Don't underestimate him, Leesie.'

I said, 'Sharpey, I'll handle it, OK?'

He said, 'Yeah, as long as you remember the rules. Tell you what. In English, they'll get you to write to your mum. Ask her for some pocket money. Tell her you're dying for a cig.'

'Thought cigs weren't allowed.'

He sighed. 'They're not, and you'll have to say that and hope she reads between the lines. But they're *needed,* see, for all sorts of reasons. Besides, visitors make a nice change, Leesie. It gets boring in here.'

Boring. Well, he was right about that.

Evenings were the worst. After Sosh, which finished at eight at the latest, you were banged up till eight next morning.

Twelve hours in a stinking cell.

With ★★★★ all to do.

No TV unless I sat next to Sharpey on his bed, which I didn't fancy. Sometimes I stood and watched, though. Sometimes I flicked through one of his mags. Sometimes I thought about how to get him for planting that spliff. Or where the next attack was coming from. But Sharpey didn't pass on any 'Craig says' and I didn't ask.

Mostly I thought about outside. That was the worst bit. What were Kirstie up to? *Who* were she doing it with? I ached thinking about her. What were my mates doing? Mum, where were she?

Sharpey told me not to worry about the spliff.

'The guvnor will just ask where you got it and dock you points when you don't tell him.'

'What if I do tell him?'

He laughed. 'They don't use thumb screws, Leesie. He's only the acting guv anyway. Won't be here long.'

'What's he like?'

'Dunno. Never seen him. I'm a good boy, Leesie. I keep out of trouble.'

He were weird. The governor I mean, though Sharpey too. The white-haired screw, Mr O'Hara I think, took me to see him next morning. His room was in the reception block and he sat behind this huge desk and hardly looked up from the paper in front of him.

'Tests have shown the article contained cannabis. Who gave it to you?'

He had a moustache like a toothbrush. A lot of the screws went in for facial hair.

I didn't tell him and he didn't insist.

He said I'd lose all privileges for fourteen days and put me on the frequent testing programme for Mandatory Drug Testing.

Then Mr O'Hara took me to the education block.

At least in classes I could start earning.

It was English first and Sharpey was right, the teacher did tell me to write to my mum. It was just like school, except that the class was smaller, only five of us, with one teacher – and a screw patrolling the corridor outside. He kept popping in to make sure we weren't attacking or ogling the teachers.

As if.

Ms Donald weren't old, but she looked like a horse. A pantomime horse. Big teeth, baggy brown top and baggy brown trousers. She even had horsetail hair. I think the aim was to disguise the fact that she was female.

The other boys were all from C-wing. Wayne, the tattoo-headed con, was one of them. Harley, the blubby one – though he weren't blubbing now – was another. Then there were two little black cons – well little compared with Errol – who had been doing sudoku in Sosh. Dead keen they were. They had seen the light, they said, and invited me to join a Bible group. Wayne just wandered round till the screw took him back to the cell. But the other three kept their heads down and so did I.

Me with the creeps, that was a first, but it didn't help. Not with letter writing. I couldn't think what to say. The page was still blank when Mr McGiven put his head round the door.

'Morrrning, Lee. Pleased to see you here.' His furry eyebrows went up, when he saw all of zilch. 'Finding it hard to find the right words, eh?'

He called the teacher over.

'Ms Donald, didn't you say Lee was an active learner?'

He explained that one of the diagnostic tests I'd done the day before showed that I learned by doing stuff, not by sitting at a desk. Well, that accounted for my success at school.

Joke.

'Right, Lee. Let's get active.' He got a chair and sat in it. 'Turn your chair round and face me. Quick. Do as you're told.'

He waited till I did.

'Good. Good. It's best not to buck the discipline, Lee. Just go along with it, till it becomes second nature.'

And I become a robot.

'Right, I'm your mother.'

What? He was talking in this daft voice.

'What would you like to say to me, Lee?'

I got up.

He said, 'Sit down.' Giving me that bayonet stare.

'It's best to co-operate, Lee.' That was Horse Face. 'We all do in this class if we want to stay in it.'

'I don't do play-acting.'

She said, 'Well, we do. We find role-play helps.'

The others had turned their chairs to watch. I didn't know where to look. This hairy great ginger screw pretending to be my mum. Another screw blocking the doorway.

So I just stood there, waiting for him to give up. See, this weren't going anywhere. But he didn't. He went on in that stupid voice.

'I'm sorry, Lee, about not coming to see you, when you were sent down, but I just couldn't face it. You've done nothing but show me up since you were little. First it was school, you either didn't go or you played up when you got there. Next it were the police knocking at the door. I warned you you'd end up inside, time and again.'

He were using her words. Well, some of them. He must have been talking to her. Behind my back.

'Well?'

I thought of the money I got for going to classes and being a good boy. 'Sorry.'

Put like that, it looks as if I just said it, but it took ages before I managed to mumble it out. Because there was no escape? Because of the money? Because I did want to see her?

'Sorry?' He looked up and then down again. 'What for exactly?'

'That I'm in this mess and caused you hassle. For . . .'

But there were things I couldn't say in front of other people. Or write down. Not for other people to read.

'Anything else to say?'

'Come and visit me? Please?'

He nodded. 'Aren't you going to ask me how I am, Lee?'

Then he was on his feet again talking in his normal voice. 'Well, that will do for a start, won't it? Sit down and get it down. Get it down. That's the secret of writing. Put it down the way you speak. Write down what you just said. Don't worry about spelling and grammar at this stage. Just write from the heart. Go on. *Dear Mum.* Just there.' He jabbed the top of the paper.

Dear Mum,

How are you? I'm sorry for all the hassle Ive caused you. I didn't mean for things to turn out like this. I hope your feeling better.

Its crap in here and I'm doing my best to get out as soon as possible.

Please come and visit me.

Miss you.

Lee

'Crap?' He was reading over my shoulder. 'What did you expect, honour among thieves?'

I wanted to ask her to bring me stuff, like Sharpey said, but couldn't think how to put it. But if she came she would, wouldn't she?

'No *love from*?' The screw was still standing there.

She didn't send no love to me.

'Miss you. That's good. Could persuade her.'

He picked it up. 'Envelope please, Ms Donald. Address it, Lee, and I'll see she gets it. Now, here's a Visiting Order.' He handed me a form. 'Put your mum's name and address on that. I'll put in a note about visiting hours and the help she can expect with travel costs.'

I was allowed one visit a fortnight, he said, on Saturday or Sunday. From up to three people. I filled in a Visiting Order for Kirstie too, and I wrote to her too.

But I didn't hold out great hopes.

Visiting time without visitors is one of the worst things inside. Even Sharpey had visitors, usually his sister. I got the cell to myself when he did, but that left me thinking about why no one visited me.

Six weeks running that happened.

Six weeks of feeling like Billy No Mates.

But then I got a letter from Kirstie!

CHAPTER 11

Dear Lee,

Thanks for your letter. Didn't know you could write!

Sorry I haven't been in touch but I've been doing overtime at the shop so as to save up so I can come and see you. I seen your mum and we are thinking of coming together. I really miss you, Lee.

I bought this nice top, your favourite colour. You'll love it.

Better be careful what I say – don't they read your letters – but it shows off my figure!!!

Will wear it when I come!!!

Love from Kirstie.

Love? Did she love me? Did I love her? Had never thought about it before. I loved doing it with her. Was that the same?

PS SEE PHOTO!

Photo?

Sharpey was dancing round the cell with it. I grabbed it off him, but then he grabbed the letter.

'Doing overtime, eh? Bet I know who with! Who d'ya thinks rogering her while you're away?'

I kept my cool.

Even when he went on and on.

Even when he told all the other cons about her.

Even when *they* went on and on.

He's making it up. He wrote it to himself. What sort of bird would date a runt like him? That sort of stuff. And worse.

I can't count the number of times I wanted to hit Sharpey. But I didn't. I was the star of Anger Management.

Kept going to other classes too. English and Maths and Strategic Thinking and Alcohol Awareness and Money Management. Anything they offered really. It earned me a bit so I could buy biscuits and shower gel. And it staved off the boredom.

There were still the long evenings though. Even longer in August because a lot of the screws were away on holiday. So we didn't always get Sosh. Sometimes it were fourteen hours in a cell at a stretch.

I even tried reading to pass the time. Horse Face gave me a book about this kid in Alcatraz. It were the same as here in some ways. The worst bit were all the hours and days and weeks just thinking about what you could be doing outside. Like doing it with Kirstie. Drinking with me mates. Playing the arcades. Or messing about on the beach.

I didn't even have no music. No iPod or CD player or nothing cos I was still on Standard and hadn't earned enough points. So Sharpey stared at his TV screen and I stared out of the window, watching the rain pouring down into the yard outside. Watching the gutters overflow and the puddles getting bigger.

There was a lot of rain that so-called summer.

The only good thing about being locked in the cell was that I saw less of Scab Face and one-eyed Craig. Only at hotplate some days. Then one night Craig didn't appear. He was on Rule 49, Sharpey said.

'Segregation. What they used to call Solitary. The Hole. Punishment block. For wrecking his cell.'

'Why'd he do that?'

Sharpey shook his head. 'You don't know nothing, do you? Even now. Sometimes it gets to you.'

I knew more than I was telling him. Sometimes I felt like banging my head against the wall.

Or his.

I knew now why there were no bog lids anywhere, or proper mirrors or chairs in the cell. Sometimes I felt like smashing stuff.

But not all cons were the same. For some, doing time were no big deal. Some of them thought inside were better than outside. Must have, cos they kept coming back. Three meals a day. A room of their own. With no effort on their part. What more could they want?

Choosing what to wear? Choosing who to be with? What and when to eat?

But it were better without Craig. I didn't get so many visits from Scab Face demanding taxes, so it were easier to keep my nose clean. I were well on my way to Enhanced, I thought, and shortening my sentence.

I were doing all right.

Till Craig returned.

Sharpey was the bearer of the good news. I'd just got back from a class when he said One-eye was back on the spur.

'And his patience is running out, Leesie. Seems he's got a job for you. Says he has mentioned this before? So I think you'd better do it. It's a question of loyalty, see.'

'Loyalty?'

'Yeah.' He didn't take his eyes off the TV screen. 'You've been playing the screws' game just lately. And you've made it too obvious, Leesie. He wants to see whose side you're on.'

Then he told me what One-eye wanted me to do.

CHAPTER 12

I felt sick.

There were none of the old excitement at the thought of nicking, because this weren't nicking. It were nastier.

Craig wanted to 'make some adjustments' to Mr Sampson's car. Mr Sampson was the bald-headed screw with the complex about it, the one I'd met on the first night. The one who called us 'young persons' – to disguise the fact he thought we were all scum.

They weren't all like that.

Making adjustments was Craig's speciality. He was in here because, among other things, he'd slit the brake hoses of an old geezer's car so that when he drove away he couldn't stop. The geezer drove into a river and drowned. Him and his dog.

Not my sort of thing.

But I did think about it. I had plenty of time to think and I were doing Strategic Thinking.

I thought about Craig's plan and decided there was no way it could work. The chances of him doing that to a screw were zero. Their cars were all locked up in a floodlit car park. We were locked up. I decided it were some sort of test, not a realistic plan, and thought of saying yes, just to get him off my back. Perhaps that was all he wanted.

But I didn't mention that to Sharpey. I let him believe I was thinking about it because I knew it would get back to One-eye.

Sharpey were very keen for me to do it.

My job was to dismantle the CCTV by cutting through the cable behind the monitor on the landing outside our cell. When the place was plunged into darkness – someone else would see to that – Craig would get into the car park. He reckoned no one would find out who did it. He was crazy.

I did show interest. 'How will I get out of the cell, Sharpey?'

He said the Asian-looking con, called Cheesey on account of his bad breath (which was saying something in that place), would open my door. At about one in the morning. All – all! – I had to do was get out of bed, climb up to the TV, cut the wire behind it. Then get back into bed.

'I'll lend you my toothbrush.'

'And what about the CCTV filming me before I dismantle it? And the screws up and down the corridor all night?'

Sharpey shook his head. 'Don't have such a negative attitude. The monitor turns. You wait till it turns away from you. And most of the night shift sleep.'

'Why can't Cheesey do the CCTV as well?'

'Cos he'll be busy letting Craig out. Then he'll be opening the gate to the car park. Look, Leesie, you need to prove yourself. Get a bit of respect. Raise your status. If you don't do your bit your life in here's gonna be hell.'

I said I could take care of myself. I'd started working out in the gym.

He said, 'You don't have to thump someone to make 'em sorry, Leesie. Think about Harley's gut ache.'

Harley was the posh kid, who had started off

all blubby, and stuck out like a boil on a bare bum. But he'd been getting on OK lately. In fact you hardly noticed him, cos he kept a low profile and had dropped his posh accent. But yesterday he'd been carted off to the sickbay, doubled up and firing at both ends.

'All because he offended Craig, Leesie. Oh dear. Have I got to spell it out again? They put shit in his dinner because he was too lippy. Remember?'

It had happened a couple of nights before during hotplate. He'd forgot for a moment he was trying to be one of the lads and started saying this place weren't too bad, no worse in fact than the posh boarding school he used to go to. Well, I saw that that went down like a fart at a vicar's tea party, but I hadn't realized he'd been dealt with.

'Shit?'

'Yeah. The brown stuff. It's the same colour as the food in here and the lippy kid weren't clever enough to spot it. So don't get on the wrong side of Craig. Do as he says.'

I thought it through again later. Used some of the thinking skills I'd learned. One of my problems and the reason I got into trouble was that I didn't think before I acted. I simply *reacted* to events. I didn't think about possible *consequences*. Grabbing Mrs Brown's handbag was a prime example. So what were my options?

Grass? Yes, I even thought of that. Result? Craig would deny it all and make my life hell.

Refuse to 'do my bit'? Ditto. Being an upright citizen in here was suicidal.

Agree to do my bit then? That might be enough if they didn't really mean to do it.

But what if they did? I'd get caught and have time added to my sentence.

In the hotplate queue that night, Craig came up behind me. 'Leesie, I want you to meet somebody.'

There was no need for introductions. The con behind him had brown skin, black hair and a bushy beard – and breath like cheese.

I said, 'I'm think—'

But was stopped by a finger over my mouth. Craig's.

'Don't think. Just do as you're told.'

So he *could* speak for himself. The eye that worked, grey as a bullet, bored into mine.

Then Errol was by my side.

And Craig's arm was behind his back. 'You leave Lee alone, One-eye, if you don't wanna lose the other one, man.'

'Step back. Step back.' The screws arrived.

Later, back in the cell, I remembered what I'd been trying to remember about Sharpey. One break, when we were kids, he'd got me to smash a fire alarm so we could rob the school tuck shop while everyone was rushing around. It worked all right for him. He got the sweets. I got caught.

He grassed me up. It were obvious now, so I'd got to be sharper than Sharpey if he weren't going to do that again.

CHAPTER 13

Sharpey went on at me all weekend about saying yes.

My life wouldn't be worth living, he said, if I didn't.

So I said yes. To shut him up. To shut Craig up. I took a chance that One-eye wouldn't really try to carry out his daft raid.

I was learning to play the game. All of their games.

That's what I thought.

Errol's was easy enough. I owed him another one now, for stepping in to help. But all he wanted was a phone card so he could phone outside for dope. His dad was a dealer who came to see him regularly. He had a lot of visitors, so Sharpey said, but I don't know how he got all the stuff in. Weren't visitors searched?

Errol just laughed when I asked him.

Sharpey said one of the screws was bent.

Still, I earned enough from going to classes to buy another phone card and let Errol have most of the credit on it. I didn't have much use for it anyhow. Mum didn't answer and I had mixed feelings about talking to Kirstie. It were all right till she went on about the great time she was having. Parties and stuff. Or about how she didn't know when she was coming to see me.

And Errol always – well, nearly always – when he weren't out of it, gave me my card back. Empty of course, but the screws didn't find out I was paying taxes.

I can't believe what an angel I was in lessons. Well, not an angel exactly but I were one of the good guys. As I've said, a new experience. I kept my mouth shut when others were shouting. I kept my head down when others were kicking the furniture. I went to more classes in there than I'd been to for the rest of my life. I learned all sorts of stuff. Like metaphors. *I was an angel.*

If that's what it took to get out of here sooner, that's what I'd do.

It helped keep me in with Mr McGiven too.

I'd got another court case coming up, for burgling a house – Mrs Brown's, if you must know. Yeah, the old lady I mugged, but it isn't as bad as it looks. I broke into her house – while she weren't there – to get some money because my mum was in debt to a loan shark on the estate called Mick. Think I mentioned that Sharpey used to do some of his dirty work for him. Well, this Mick said if she didn't pay him back pronto he'd 'sort her out'.

Anyway, I needed a good report from Mr McGiven to avoid getting another year added to this one. A longer sentence? I could handle it, but I didn't want to.

Sharpey was right about one thing, I decided. You had to keep in with everyone. It was like juggling. You had to keep all your balls in the air – and take care someone didn't knock you to the floor and kick them in at the same time.

Joke? I remember when I told them all the time.

I didn't take all Sharpey's advice though and I didn't obey all the rules.

Underneath his shirt, Sharpey had more cuts than a butcher's block. We were supposed to grass on each other about that. The screws called it 'looking out for each other'. They must have known what he did from the health checks, but they didn't know how he did it. I could have told them, and where he hid his blade.

The screws searched the cells every day – different times – but they never found it. They had the mattresses off the beds. They examined every inch. They had all his pictures off the walls. They emptied bottles of cleaning fluid down the sink.

But they didn't look in his special toothbrush. Because he didn't hide it. It was in his home-made toothbrush holder.

The whole cutting business made me feel sick. Can't stand the sight of blood. But Sharpey said I'd regret it if I grassed.

He offered to show me how to make my own instrument. First, hold back a safety razor one morning. The screws counted them out and counted them in every morning, but it was easy, he said, to cause a bit of confusion and nick one.

I weren't so sure. Some screws were easier to confuse than others. They weren't all the same when you got to know them a bit.

But back to Sharpey's special toothbrush. He said you got some thread out of something you were wearing. Nylon was best and you could usually find a loose one in your tracksuit. Then you wound it round the razor to fix it in the middle of the bristles. Or you could get a cig and melt the plastic and fix it that way. You also had to give up cleaning your teeth. Cutting relieved the tension, Sharpey said.

I said I preferred wanking. He said he did that as well. I said I knew. I could hear him grunting at night. The sheets stank of stale spunk.

It was bad. I even found myself fantasizing about Horse Face sometimes. That's how desperate I got.

But I were coping. And things looked up when I got another letter from Kirstie to say her and Mum were coming to visit. In three days' time, on Saturday afternoon!

Sharpey said she were winding me up.

'She won't come. She's got better things to do.'

But I could hardly keep still.

CHAPTER 14

They were late though, and I'd started to think Sharpey were right. It had been like Clapham Junction on the landing for about half an hour. Doors opening and closing, keys turning, screws' feet clunking up and down. And Sharpey had been one of the first to go. Anyway there I was, Billy No Mates again I thought, when Mr Sampson opened the cell door and handed me one of the red bibs.

'Put that on, Lee, and proceed to Visiting.'

I said, 'Who's visiting me, Mr Sampson?'

I still couldn't believe it.

He said, 'Don't know, Lee. Who would?'

Sometimes I could see why One-eye had it

in for him. Then it was all quick march and no chat across the yard, past the window warriors with their faces pressed against the glass. Poor sods. I actually felt sorry for them.

I could have run across that yard.

But when I got there – he headed for the education block – my guts started churning.

A classroom had been re-arranged for visitors, with tables in rows. Each table had one or two chairs by it. Full, all of them. That's what I first thought. But no Kirstie. No Mum.

It was a mistake. Or a wind up. They weren't really coming.

Then Mr Sampson pointed out an empty table in the middle of the room with three chairs at it, two one side, one the other.

'Sit down, Lee.' He went out again.

Errol was there. So was Stumpy and Scab Face and One-eye. And screws of course, watching. As I said, half the spur and their visitors.

But I still couldn't believe mine would come.

Then the door opened and there was Kirstie coming towards me. She looked *gorgeous*. Even more good-looking than I remembered. Honest. There was an intake of breath when she came in. All heads turned to look at her. Her golden hair was all long and bouncy and she was wearing this turquoise top.

Low cut!

The blonde short-haired female screw brought her and Mum to my table.

And I didn't know what to say.

Still couldn't believe it.

Felt my eyes filling up.

Why? It was the best thing that had happened for weeks. I found a tissue in my pocket and blew my nose. Said something about having a cold.

She laughed.

Because I couldn't keep still? I didn't know where to put myself. Not that I had to make that decision. But Mr Nobby was jumping around, even before Kirstie leaned over the table and gave me a kiss.

'In the netball team, are you?' She were laughing at the daft bib.

I tried not to drool like some sex-starved idiot. But she looked so good and I hadn't seen a decent-looking bird for weeks and I wanted to tear off the stupid bib and everything else. Would have if we'd been alone. But there were a table between us. And loads of other cons watching. And screws.

And Mum. 'Shall I leave you two together?'

Being inside turns you into a muppet.

Kirstie said, 'Aren't you gonna say hello to your mum, Lee?'

'Hello, Mum.'

She wrinkled her nose. 'It smells in here. Doesn't anyone wash?'

'Not a lot.' I had to laugh. Same old Mum then. Moan moan moan. About everything. The screw searching her, and not being allowed to have a cig, and how long it had taken to get here. And . . .

And I gazed at Kirstie who eventually managed to get a word in edgeways.

'We bought you some cigs, Lee, but they took them off us. Said they weren't allowed. They took everything off us. Can't believe it. I'd downloaded some Trance onto a CD.'

I said, 'Thanks' and 'It's the thought that counts,' and didn't say I hadn't got nothing to play it on. Trance. That would keep the pipe-banging out of my head. But all I wanted to do was get my hands on her.

Not just my hands.

But now her eyes were all over the place.

I said, 'Seen someone you like better?' But I

don't think she heard. Mum was still going on about everything being all my fault.

'I lost my job, Lee, because of you. The boss said I'd had too much time off work.'

I said, 'I'll make it up to you, right?'

Honest, I was so happy I could have kissed her too. I was going to say about training and getting a job and helping her out but Kirstie decided to give us her attention.

'Aren't you going to tell your mum how nice she looks, Lee? She's been to Spain.'

'Spain?'

'That's where the cigs came from. Two hundred duty frees.'

Two hundred cigs! But it was the going to Spain that knocked me for six.

I said, 'How, when you got no money?'

'I had the ticket I bought for you to go to Bob's.'

'You used my ticket?'

'Well, you couldn't and it was going out of date.'

Kirstie chipped in again. 'You should be pleased for her, Lee. It gave her a nice break.'

'I *am* pleased.' *Lie.* So that's why she never

answered my calls. But she did look better. Tanned, and sort of, not happy exactly, but better.

But that could have been *me* in Spain! The ticket was *mine!*

Bob was Mum's brother. He was a builder and he'd offered me a job on a building site. I'd have been there now if I hadn't got banged up.

Think positive.

Self Talk – to perk yourself up and get things clear in your head – was something I learned about in Problem Solving.

I said, 'Did you talk to Uncle Bob about my job?'

'Sort of.' She bit her bottom lip.

'What did he say?'

'He weren't keen, Lee, not with you having a record and that.'

Great.

'He never liked your dad.'

'What's that got to do with it?'

She didn't answer.

Just like your dad. Just like your dad.

I said, 'I'm going to change, right?'

'And pigs might fly, Lee.'

Thanks, Mum, shall I top myself now?

Kirstie said, 'What's it like in here?'

I said, 'Fantastic. A holiday camp.'

'Oh, good. I knew you'd be all right. Scorpio. Ruled by Pluto, god of the underworld.' She went back to gazing round the room and I remembered exactly why I had another court case coming up.

I broke into Mrs Brown's house to get the money to pay for *that ticket to Spain*. Mum had borrowed from Mick to buy it. Not that I'd asked her. It was her idea to ask her brother to give me a job. Anyway, Mick suddenly said he wanted the money back. Pronto. I think he was relying on me to pay him back by doing a job for him, and when he heard I had a court case coming up, for mugging Mrs Brown, he thought I'd go down before he got his money back.

Anyhow, he told me he'd *sort her out* if he didn't get his money. *I* had to get it. Fast. Before the court case. Well, I knew what his sortings out were, so I did. She wouldn't be looking so good now if I hadn't.

I said, 'I needn't even have burgled Mrs Brown's house. There was another way, you know.'

It was one of the Alternative Actions I'd thought of in Problem Solving. 'You could have cashed in that ticket. Got your money back and repaid him.'

She stood up. 'Hindsight's great, Lee. I don't think they do give you your money back and sorry, but I've got to have a cig.'

One of the screws came over and escorted her out. But at least Kirstie managed to tear her eyes away from Errol.

I said, 'Fancy him?'

She said, 'It's not him, it's the little black baby. She's so cute. I'd love a little baby like that.'

I didn't say the obvious.

Errol was dancing a baby girl up and down on the table, and Kirstie weren't the only one watching. Half the room was.

The other half were looking at Kirstie.

The baby was laughing and shrieking and now *everyone* was looking at her. Even the screws. Stumpy was clapping his hands and his brothers – I thought they must be his brothers – were laughing at him.

Kirstie said, 'She's all matching, Lee. Pink dress, pink bows, everything.'

I said, 'I'd rather look at you. She looks like a hedgehog.'

The kid's hair was in plaits sticking out of her head in all directions.

Kirstie laughed. 'Do you think that's her mum?'

'Who?'

'The lady with her. Wearing that costume?'

'Nah. Looks like Mother Theresa.' Except that she was black. But she was wearing a white dress like a nun, with green borders, though, and she had a big wooden cross hanging from her waist. 'And she's too old.'

It was Errol's old lady, his mum, the baby's granny, we all learned next day in Sosh. The baby was his. His little girl. Dead proud of her, he was. Her name was Amy-Jane.

'What your old lady bring you?' I'm not sure who asked.

'Sweets,' he said and everyone fell about. 'And holy books.'

I thought they were going to wet themselves with laughing. But when he said he was telling the truth and insisted she hadn't brought any ganja, the smile left their faces.

'But she brought the baby, man. Everyone knows that's the best way of bringing stuff in. They don't like to search babies.' That was Craig.

'Don't search babies.' That was Scab Face.

'They do, man.'

'They don't. I bet your little girl was carrying

loads of stuff in her nappy and you're like keeping it to yourself.'

When Craig said that I saw a nerve in Errol's face jump. I saw his fists clench. I knew he was getting mad. But they didn't see it. Or maybe they did. Anyway they kept on. Well, Craig did and Scab Face did, because Scab Face did everything that Craig did and more. Like a parrot.

And Craig didn't see the warning signs. Since his spell in solitary he'd been even thicker. Don't think banging his head against the wall did him any good. His face was still covered with yellowing bruises.

Errol said, 'You like keep quiet about my little girl, One-eye. It's my old man brings the stuff, innit?'

Now Craig tensed up. It didn't do to mention his eye.

'You were jigging her up and down, Black Boy. Bet you were shaking it out.'

'My little girl in't no mule!'

'Go suck . . .'

Now the screws moved in. 'Cool it. Separate. Step back.'

But they were too late.

Scab Face said something I didn't hear and

Errol wasn't thinking about the Rules for Cool. He wasn't counting to ten or taking deep breaths. Anger Management wasn't his thing. His great fist shot out. I think he went for Craig, but Scab Face must have stepped in front because he caught it on the nose.

It didn't do anyone any good.

'Rule 49!' The screws grabbed them both.

They both – Errol and Scab Face – got Segregation and that's where Errol's life took a downturn.

Mine too, though it didn't look that way at first.

CHAPTER 15

In fact things looked better for a bit.

Hotplate was cancelled for a week, and we had to eat cold grub in our cells. But I weren't too bothered about that because with Errol gone, I got my own cell at last and could eat in peace.

No cloud without a silver!

Same great décor as the other one, but at least I didn't have to witness Sharpey slicing himself or any of his other activities. And he couldn't see mine. It weren't privacy exactly, but it were better than sharing.

It was good being able to read a postcard from Kirstie without him looking over my shoulder. Even if she were only saying it took them four hours to get home. Didn't hear from Mum but she had left me a few quid which smoothed things along. Not that I got it all straightaway. The screws doled it out when they saw fit, but that was OK. The longer it lasted, the better. Couldn't see Mum coming again in a hurry.

Or Kirstie. But I could put her photo on the wall.

It was Errol's old cell and the smell of ganja in it was so strong I think it made me high. Was that what raised my spirits? The screws must have turned a blind eye – or nose – to his smoking. I breathed so much of it in, I was a bit worried about the next urine test.

Note my clean vocabulary! I were – was – learning so fast. Horse Face said I might be able to do GCSE English one day if I kept at it.

My drug-free urine was a valuable commodity. A nice little earner. Everyone wanted it. It wasn't too difficult to substitute some of mine for theirs. So I was more than a bit worried that it might get contaminated.

Errol wasn't doing well. That's what I heard. When he came off Rule 49 he was moved to a different spur. Soon after that he got a letter from his mum saying she weren't bringing Amy-Jane to see him any more. She didn't want her contaminated by all the evil inside. I could see her point. Inside was no place for a little girl. But I could also see she was getting at Errol where it hurt most.

He loved that little girl. He even went to Child Care classes.

I carried on doing all right. It was easier in my own cell and I'd nearly got enough points and dosh to buy a CD player. Cheap one. So I could listen to the CD Kirstie had made for me. And I was shortening my sentence.

If only I hadn't got the other case coming up. Best not to think about it.

Then Sonia appeared one morning and I had to. Think about it, I mean. She was in Mr McGiven's room when I arrived for my weekly meeting. She sat behind his desk. He stood by her, watching, bayonet poised, well not really, but you know what I mean.

Sonia had a date for my case, she said. November 1st. A week before my eighteenth birthday.

'I've been to see your mum, Lee, and she advises you, to er . . . make a clean breast of it.'

She did see the funny side of it, I could tell,

but it weren't a good idea saying it. I didn't hear her for the next five minutes. She was wearing this fluffy blue polo-necked sweater and . . .

'Calm down, lad.' Mr McGiven took a step forward. He had a grin on his face too. 'Ms Benson asked you to tell her exactly what happened. OK?'

'Why? Don't I get someone proper to defend me?'

'Yes. You'll have a solicitor, but Ms Benson's pre-sentence report will carry a lot of weight. She will also speak up for you in court – if she can – so you need to make a statement.'

She had a laptop in front of her, fingers poised over the keyboard. Prompted by her questions, I told her everything, being as honest as I could.

'On the 27th June I went round to Mrs Brown's house.'

'Intending to rob her?'

'Yes.'

'A premeditated crime?' She frowned.

'Yes. Ken – he runs the community centre – told me she was so scared of me she had gone to stay with her sister, so the house was empty.'

'But not so that you'd go round and rob her?' She shook her head. 'It's not looking good, Lee, but go on.'

'I was desperate.'

'Why?'

I told her about Mum being in debt to a loan shark and him saying if she didn't pay him back he'd 'sort her out.'

'Beat her up. That's what he meant. He said if I didn't get him the money fast, he'd make sure I did. Go down, I mean.'

'How would he do that?' Sonia was looking straight at me.

I looked at the floor. Couldn't meet her eye.

'How would he do that?' She said it again.

He said he'd tell the court that I'd beat up my mum and prove I was violent. A danger to the community.

But I couldn't say it.

Couldn't say I hit my mum.

That's why I was determined that she wouldn't get hurt again.

Just thinking about it made me feel sick. More than anything I've ever done, I wish I hadn't done that. It made me feel like something floating in the karzy.

But I'd been so mad.

Mad. Angry. Furious. Words don't describe the feeling. People talk of seeing red but it's nowhere near right. When Mick – he were the loan shark – said Mum had a boyfriend and was spending all her money on him I didn't see red, I *felt* red. I were burning. It was like a fire inside me flaring up and roaring through me – right into my fists.

And feet.

Up to then I'd been trying so hard to go straight, so I could get a good report and go to Spain and get a job and not be sent down and now *she'd* ruined everything. *She'd* got me in this fix.

With a boyfriend. Yeah, that was part of it too.

I don't remember going home, up the stair-ways and stuff, just bursting in and shouting at her, and her going for me, and me going back at her, shaking her till she fell on the ground and then . . .

I kicked her.

'Concentrate, Lee.' Mr McGiven was by my side. 'Ms Benson just asked you a question.'

In the face.

She didn't tell me till afterwards, when she was on the floor crying, holding her head, that it weren't for a boyfriend. She hadn't got a boyfriend. It was *me* she'd borrowed the money for. To buy a ticket to Spain.

I felt like shit. Still do.

Scum. Worse. There aren't words.

I couldn't believe what I'd done. Knew I'd blown it. I'd have given anything to undo it, but life isn't a video you can wind back.

I wanted to put my arms round her, like I did when Dad had hit her. But she were screaming at me not to come near her.

'Get out of my sight. YOU'RE JUST LIKE YOUR DAD!'

And she were right.

I'd turned into him.

I'd turned into my dad.

Sonia pushed a box of tissues towards me.

If that got out inside, my life wouldn't be worth living. Mugging an old lady made me pretty low in the heap. Beating up my own mum would put me right at the bottom. All the cons made a big thing about looking after their old ladies. Say something about a con's mum and you were dead meat. They all made out they were knights in shining armour. None of them would do such a thing. Or so they said.

Sonia said, 'The burglary, Lee. Try to concentrate. You didn't just take money. You took Mrs Brown's jewellery box as well. Yes?'

'I was in a rush. I didn't know if there was enough cash. I hoped he'd take it in kind.'

'And did he?'

'Yes. I had to do something, anything to stop him hurting my mum.'

I sounded as if butter wouldn't melt.

But it were true. I didn't want her hurt again – not by that low life.

Sonia typed away for a bit.

'Now, Lee, Mrs Brown, your victim, is very upset about losing her engagement ring and her bracelet. They were presents from her husband – before he died. How do you feel about that?'

'Haven't thought about it.'

'Well, that's honest, but you need to. Put yourself in her shoes. Think about how *she* felt. Then write a letter to her saying how sorry you are. You're expressing – and seem to be feeling – remorse for something. I've been watching you, Lee. You're really upset. That's good and it will help. A letter to your victim could be read out in court as evidence that you've changed.'

She said the court wanted to see evidence of the three Rs: Remorse, Rehabilitation and Reparation. 'Remorse is being sorry for what you've done. Rehabilitation is becoming a useful member of society. Reparation is repairing the damage you've done. Mr McGiven says you're working hard on the rehab. Now if you could tell the police how to get Mrs Brown's jewellery back that would count as Reparation and help a lot.'

Grass on Mick? She had to be joking. He wouldn't even need Sharpey to tell him I'd done it. But he'd get Sharpey to sort me out inside. And he'd be waiting for me when I got outside.

Mr McGiven chipped in. 'This is very important, Lee. If you don't get this right you could spend your *nineteenth* birthday in prison and even your twentieth. Real prison. This loan shark – and fence – he sounds like a nasty piece of work. You'd be doing a lot of people a favour if you shopped him. Sounds as if the Churchill estate would be well rid of him.'

'That's good advice.' Sonia stood up and started packing her briefcase. 'It would help your case.'

Mr McGiven said, 'Right, we've agreed you'll write a letter to Mrs Brown expressing remorse, and saying you'll try to get her jewellery back? Yes? Yes?' He gave me that bayonet stare.

'Yeah.'

'Good man.' He opened a file on his desk.

'It's time you chose some training courses and started preparing for life outside. If you do what we suggest, the magistrate might look on you kindly.'

'Oh yeah?'

'Magistrates do try to be fair, Lee. If they think you've learned your lesson they won't see any point in adding to your sentence. Let's be hopeful, shall we? *Hope is a good thing and good things never die?* Yes, Ms Benson?'

'Definitely.'

It all sounded too good to be true.

And you know what they say about that.

CHAPTER 16

Mr McGiven never stopped trying.

He turned up to my next English lesson. 'Now, this letter to Mrs Brown, have you written it yet?'

I shook my head.

'Thought not, but you ought to get on with it. October already. Your case is only a month away. Now, this might help.'

He waved a handbag.

I *could* believe it. The man was a nutter.

What was he up to now? I hoped he weren't going to start play acting. But he sat down and called the rest of the class over. There were five of us: posh Harley, who didn't sound so posh these days; Wayne, the one with tattoos all over his head; and the two black cons – Leroy and Winston – who were always so head-down keen. They were working away with headphones over their ears, but Horse Face, Ms Donald, fetched them over and told them to take them off.

'Come on. You can all do this.' Mr McGiven waited till we were sitting round the table. Then he started talking about '*an* old lady', the victim of a mugger, and for a horrible moment I thought he was going to tell the whole room what I'd done. 'Now, this is what she lost when she was mugged.'

He emptied the bag onto the table.

'It was all in there. Look, her wedding ring, a picture of her brother when he was a young man, a library book, a doctor's prescription, her keys, her pension book. And cash. What the mugger really wanted. Oh, and her reading glasses.'

He spread them out.

'Now, which of these things do you think she missed most?'

Harley said, 'The cash.'

'Think about it.' Mr McGiven got up. 'Discuss it. You'll all need to put yourself in the old lady's place. Imagine you were her. She lived alone. She was a bit rheumaticky – your fingers swell up when you get old – so she couldn't wear her wedding ring. Her husband died a few years back. Her brother died a long time ago in the war. That's a very old photo and not very clear, but you didn't get many in those days.'

He stood up.

'I'll leave them with you. While I'm out of the room, you have a think about how she would *feel*? Discuss it and put the items in order – one to eight – according to how much she missed them.'

The others started arguing. I kept quiet in case I gave myself away, but I did try to think. A wedding ring? Most people didn't get married these days. Don't bother with wedding rings and stuff. It were different then, I suppose. The ring could have reminded her of when he asked her to marry him and stuff like that and getting married and the good times they'd had together. Though it might make her feel worse. Miss him more.

A ring. That's all I've got now. I was surprised at the words in my head, and had only just moved on to the photo when Mr McGiven came back. Even the others hadn't got very far.

He picked up the pension book. 'Would she miss this?'

'Yes, but she could get another.' That was Wayne.

'How?'

'Go to the post office. Fill in a form.'

Mr McGiven picked up her glasses. 'Without these? And how long will it be before it comes even if she gets someone to fill it in for her?'

'Ages if it's like the Giro.'

'She could get new glasses.'

'How's she going to pay for them?'

'She's got more money in her house.'

He picked up the keys.

'How's she going to get into her house?'

I said something about getting another key cut. He said, 'Yes if she's left a spare with a neighbour, but again how's she going to pay for it? Her money's gone. Her pension book's gone.'

I said, 'We're going round in circles.'

He said, 'How d'you think she's feeling?'

'That she's going round in circles. She don't know what to do first. She's all het up and upset.'

He nodded and picked up the old photo. 'And what about this?'

It were a young man in an army uniform. 'Can she get a new one of these?'

No one answered.

'Why do you think she kept that photo?'

'To help remember her brother.' That was Harley.

'Why?'

'Because she wanted to.'

'Why, Harley?'

'Because she loved him.'

Mr McGiven nodded. He made you say stuff like that.

'So how do you think the old lady is feeling as she sits in her hospital bed. She can't read her library book to take her mind off it. She can't read anything without her glasses. She can't look at photos to remind her of happier times.'

'Crap.'

'Yes, Lee, but try and think of another word. And then she's got her injuries. Cuts and bruises. The mugger pushed her to the ground when she held onto her bag. She's hurting.'

'Double crap.' The others laughed, but they wouldn't have if they knew.

'And how do you think she'll feel about going out to get her pension next time, if she does get it all sorted?'

I let someone else answer that.

'Scared. That it might happen again. She won't want to step out the door.'

'Yes, she's afraid to go out and afraid to stay in because the mugger's got her key. He might break in and attack her. What's it like feeling that you can't trust anyone, that your property isn't safe and that someone might attack you at any moment?'

I knew exactly how that felt.

'Do you think people should have to feel like that?

I shook my head.

'What do you think she'd most like to get back?'

'All of it.'

He nodded. 'All of you, imagine you're that mugger and write your letter to the old lady.' He said, 'all of you' but it were me he was talking to, me who was doing it for real.

Dear Mrs Brown

You probly don't want to hear from me, but please don't tear up this letter before you read it. I know, words are cheap, but I want to say I'm sorry for what I did to you. When I grabbed your bag, I was showing off in front of my mates. I told them it would be a piece of ... well, easy. I didn't think about your feelings. Or the consequences. I didn't think youd hang onto it. All my mates were jeering. Me being stopped by an old lady and I lost it. Gave you a push and you fell and hurt your head. I never intended none of that. I admit I wanted your money at the time, but I feel really bad that you got hurt and lost all your other precious things and had to go to hospital.

I'm sorry about breaking in later too and taking more stuff.

Anyway, I'm serving my time for what I did. I've had plenty of time to think about things and the more I think about it the more sorry I am. I'm learning to think before I act and go to Anger Management.

The Anger Management was going really well. I knew the Rules for Cool – short term and long term – off by heart. Somehow I'd managed not to thump anyone all the time I'd been inside. And it weren't for lack of provocation. Worse since they'd seen Kirstie. Dead jealous, they never stopped trying to wind me up. Sharpey said he had 'inside' knowledge that she was seeing someone else.

But I didn't take his bait.

Don't blame other people. Don't let them get to you.

I did loads of Self Talk like that. Sounds barmy, talking to yourself, but it helps. Anyway, back to the letter.

I realize it was wrong to take your stuff. I know how you feel. I don't like it when people take mine.

Had enough of that in here. The phone card was only the beginning. Some thieving sod had had my photo of Kirstie.

It was brave of you to hang onto it but I wish you hadn't. I wish none of this had happened. One thing just led to another.

And another and another. It's all very well for Mr McGiven to talk about choice, as if it's all up to me. He's no idea what it's like living on the Churchill estate. I wrote a whole page, but I hadn't finished by the end of the lesson, so I took it back to the cell and carried on.

Your probly thinking I'm saying all this because the other case is coming up, for breaking into your house. Well in a way your right, but that doesn't mean I'm not sorry. I do feel bad making you scared to stay in your own home. I broke in because I needed the money to pay my mums debts. This sounds like an excuse but it isn't it's a reason, and there wasn't enough cash so I took your jewlry. She owed a man some money and he said he would beat her up if I didn't pay him back. Straitaway.

Mick a man? He was a form of low life.

Anyway I had to get the money so my mum wouldnt get hurt. I am not an angel but I do not go round hurting women, Well not on purpose. Well, only when I lose it and I'm working on that.

It's wrong to steal but it seemed the only thing to do at the time.

I hope you are feeling better

Yours sincerely,

Lee mercer

Two pages! And after a lot of thought I added a PS

PS When I get out I'll try and get your jewlry back.

Reparation too! I felt real good as I folded it neatly and put it in my pocket to give to Mr McGiven later. But it was a mistake.

I'd forgotten about Sharpey.

CHAPTER 17

It was Mr Sampson's fault as well.

He was losing his grip. Word was his wife had left him. Anyway, he'd switched to day shift. Or maybe he was doing overtime.

'Shower,' he grunted next morning, when he opened up. Not his usual 'Morning' or 'Rise and shine'.

It was a Saturday – no classes – and he let us out three at a time.

'You lot stink.'

We weren't 'young persons' any more either.

The shower block was between the two spurs of C-wing and there were six cubicles with stable doors. No privacy. For our own protection, the screws said.

He said, 'Strip off and leave your clothes outside. I'll keep an eye.'

But he didn't keep an eye. Couldn't stand the smell most like. Think mouldy walls, manky socks and drains. He just left us to it. Or maybe he got a call on his radio. I don't know, but I was in the middle stall and Harley and Wayne were either side.

And Sharpey was on the loose, though I didn't know it.

I'd seen him earlier on the landing with some other cons, when a screw was taking them to the yard for exercise. They were heading downstairs. But he must have got back somehow and got his hands in my pocket.

Because he got the letter I'd written.

It weren't till I saw him later, on the landing, that I saw what he'd done. I was outside my door. He was leaning against the rail, shaking his head.

Reading it.

Mr Sampson was busy banging up Wayne and Harley. Another screw was taking more cons to the showers. One-eye, Craig, was one of them with Scab Face and a new con. Their screw stopped to speak to Mr Sampson, who forgot he was supposed to be locking me up, and One-eye said something to Scab Face, who sidled over to me.

'Not long now.'

Afterwards I realized he was talking about his daft plan. But I took no notice at the time. I was thinking about how to handle Sharpey.

He was holding my letter at arm's length over the rail and I went up to him as calmly as I could.

He said, 'You can't send this, Leesie.'

I said, 'Gimme that.'

He started shaking his head from side to side, slowly like, sighing and sucking his lip, while looking at my letter. And I felt the anger rising. Felt myself getting hotter. Felt my heart beating faster.

Don't let him wind you up. I tried Self Talk.

I practised Self Control.

I carried out the Rules for Cool to the letter.

1. I unclenched my fists.

2. I took deep breaths and counted to 10, letting my breath out on 11.

3. I walked away. (Well, I stepped back, trying

to look casual, as if I didn't care. But my pulses were racing.)

4. I communicated assertively but not aggressively. (Though my leg were twitching.)

'Why not, Sharpey? What's wrong with it? Not that you should be reading my letter.'

I kept my voice down, knowing all the others would be at their doors, straining to hear.

But he wanted everyone to hear. All the cons, anyway. The screws had done one of their vanishing acts.

'It's you I'm thinking about, Leesie. Send this you'll hang yourself. You're admitting everything, like. They'll read this out in court, see. Everyone will know what you did before. It'll go against you.'

'They know anyhow. I have a record, remember?'

'But' – he wagged his finger – 'they can only look at one case at a time. Right?'

I weren't sure about that.

'Well, take it from Sharpey, they can. Now, listen cos I'm trying to help like. You're up for burglary, right? Well, don't go round reminding the whole court that you mugged the same old lady a few weeks earlier. That'll prove to them you're heartless. A no-hoper. A persistent offender. You'll be off to clink, big time. Another thing. What do you mean saying you'll try and get the old lady's foolery back?'

I thought hard before I answered. I didn't want to provoke him. I just wanted that letter back.

I said, 'When I get out I'll go and see Mick, that's all. Ask him what he did with it.'

'He'll have passed the stuff on by now.'

'I know. I'll ask him who he sold it to?'

He raised a scabby eyebrow. 'You're not thinking of grassing him up, are you?'

'No.'

'Cos that wouldn't be wise. Mick don't let anyone dob him.'

Well, you should know.

I didn't say that. I was a model of restraint.

Too restrained. Too slow. He side-stepped into his cell before I could get my hands on my letter.

I hammered on his door. 'Sharpey, that's mine.'

No answer, only Stumpy in his cell saying, 'Is anything the matter, Lee?'

I said, 'Sharpey, that letter is my private property.'

No answer.

Not a screw in sight. I lifted the hatch and

there was the rodent tearing my letter into little pieces. Then I heard the karzy flushing and there was nothing I could do.

Then.

He came up to me later in Sosh when I was having a game of pool with Stumpy. I'd seen him making a phone call.

'Got a message from Mick.'

'What a coincidence.' I managed to pot a red, though my pulses were racing.

'I'm trying to help, right. Got any cigs?'

'No.'

'Anyway, Mick says don't say where you got rid of the old girl's stuff. *Don't* mention his name or where he hangs out like. If the feds start sniffing round, he'll get someone round your mum's so fast she won't know what hit her. Hit her. Get it? It would be such a shame if your mummy got hurt. Again.'

He smirked. There was everything in that smirk.

And I wanted to wipe it off his face.

I could feel my breathing getting faster, feel the fire inside flaring and roaring. Feel it racing towards my fists.

I took a deep breath.

I unclenched my fists.

I started counting.

One.

Two.

Three.

Four.

Five.

Six.

Seven.

Eight.

Nine.

'Same goes for you, of course, Leesie. Mick will be waiting for you when you get outside. On the other hand, if you play Mick's game, he says he could find you a job when you come out. He could use someone like you. If you're big enough to hit *blokes* that is.'

Ten.

I hit him, right between his nasty bulging ferrety little eyes.

CHAPTER 18

It was worth a week on Rule 49.

It was worth losing points.

I enjoyed it, hitting Sharpey that is. I was not sorry I did it. Does that make me a psychopath?

Rule 49. Segregation From Others and Withdrawal of Privileges. They don't call it Solitary anymore. Public Relations. Too many cons in Solitary have topped themselves. But same difference. You're on your own 24/7 except for one visit a day from a screw and the chaplain and a nurse. You can do sweet FA except stare at the bare walls and you don't mix with other cons.

You can't watch TV or play games. You can't

go to classes or the gym. You can't phone anyone – except the Samaritans. But I didn't feel suicidal. Not mixing was fine.

Till the pictures started crowding into my head. Of Mum's eye changing from red to purple to yellow. Of Mick waiting outside. Of Dad hitting Mum. Dad hitting me. Me hitting Sharpey.

Was that such a good idea? What good did it do? What did it prove? That I hadn't changed. That I could still lose it. That other people could make me lose it. That they were in control.

Just like your dad.

I saw how it could happen. Thirty seconds of rage. Thirty years inside. *Just like your dad. Just like your dad. Just like your dad. Just like your dad. Just like your dad . . .*

So when the door opened and Mr McGiven came in, mouth down to his ever so shiny shoes, it was almost a relief.

'All rrrrrright.' He groaned as he sat down. 'What happened? Tell me. Everrrrrrrything.'

'Sharpey riled me and I hit him.'

'How? Why?'

End of conversation. That one anyhow. He went on about how I'd managed to control my temper for weeks now, though I must have been riled before.

'So why lose it now, Lee? Why this backward step?'

I didn't say anything. Couldn't. Sharpey and Mick had me in a double bind. If I said anything against them it would get back to them, and my mum would get it. If I didn't say anything they might leave her alone, but they'd think they had me by the short and curlies.

They did. I was their prisoner, inside or out.

He asked if I'd finished the letter to Mrs Brown.

I said, 'No.'

'But it was going so well. Where is it now, back in your cell?'

I didn't say anything. I didn't grass.

Mr McGiven stroked his moustache. 'Was this dispute with Sharpey anything to do with the letter?'

Could he see inside my head? More likely he knew cons inside out. Anyhow, he said that he'd try and get me some paper and a pen to write another one.

Mr Sampson came in later with a sheet of paper and a pencil. Eyes glaring, he just handed it over without a word. It was an extra, see. You weren't supposed to get extras on Rule 49.

Not when you'd just thumped someone – on his watch.

Dear Mrs Brown

I began. There was nothing else to do and plenty of time to think about what to say.

I know you probly don't want to hear from me, but please don't tear this up before you read it. I want to say I'm sorry for what I did to you. I feel realy bad about robbing you because I know what it feels like when people take your property away from you. I wish I could get it back for you, but I can't, though I'll pay you back the money if – when – I get a job. Most of all I'm sorry for making it so you're afraid to stay in your own home. I know what that's like too.

I remembered hiding from my dad. *Just like your dad.* Under the bedclothes. *Just like your dad.* Pretending to be asleep but shaking so much he knew I weren't. Him dragging me out and . . .

'NO! I'M–NOT–LIKE–HIM!'

The words screamed out of me making my throat sore.

Or maybe that were the blubbing.

Because I had hit my mum.

And I'd pushed Mrs Brown, an old lady who couldn't defend herself, because she'd hung onto her bag.

And Sharpey.

I wrote more.

I broke in because I needed the money to pay my mums debts, and there wasn't enough cash so I took your jewlry as well. Anyway I had to get the money. It seemed the only thing to do at the time. It were a spur of the moment thing. I know better now and I won't do anything like that again.

But how do I know I won't? Self Talk. It can drive you mad.

I showed the letter to Mr McGiven next day.

'Mmmm.' More moustache stroking. 'Not as good as your first draft. It's lost something. You've said sorry. You've shown a certain amount of remorse, but . . .'

He read it again.

'What about reparation? I thought you were going to say you were going to try and get her jewellery back? By telling the police about the thug who terrorizes the estate?'

'I didn't say that.'

'But you were thinking about it?'

'Yeah, well.'

'And?'

'I can't.'

'Lee, you don't have to name the fence in the letter. Just tell me, and say in your letter you'll do your best to get her jewellery back.'

We were going round in circles.

'Are you frrrr–ightened of something, Lee?'

Do dogs poo . . .?

I thought carefully about what I could safely say.

'This fence if I grass him up, he's said he'll sort out my mum.'

'If he was inside he couldn't.'

'He would get someone else to do it. And how long would it take them to put him inside? How long would it take the police to pick him up? How long before his case came up? And what would he do in the meantime?'

I explained that the feds don't exactly rush to places like the Churchill estate when they get a 999 call. I'm not sure Mum would bother to make one. She hadn't got much faith in the feds.

I *didn't* name Mick, but I did explain that if the feds caught up with him they'd find it hard to fix anything on him. If it came to court he'd probably get off. He'd get good lawyers. Then he'd be after me and Mum. If he hadn't got to her first.

He said, 'That's a very negative view.'

I said, 'It's the Churchill estate not *Heartbeat*.'

He looked thoughtful. I'll give him that.

'Well, have a look at this while you're in here.'

It was the list of training courses that you could do when you had a release date.

I handed it back.

He went on about keeping hopeful. 'Construction. Didn't you say your uncle was a builder in Spain? Weren't you going to work for him?"

'Yes, but he's withdrawn his offer on account of my having a criminal record. And being my father's son.'

He looked at his watch. 'This hasn't gone as well as I hoped, Lee.'

He handed back my letter. 'Think about this again if you don't want time added to your sentence. Burglary is a serious crime. You need to make a good impression in court to avoid being sent to an adult prison.'

He stood up. 'You wouldn't like it, Lee. We try here – to help you change your way of life. Educate you. In prison too, but it's more about punishment there. But it's your choice.'

He still hadn't got a clue. It were then that I started to see why some cons can't see the point of carrying on.

Shit or shit. That was the choice.

CHAPTER 19

When I got back to the spur there was more
bad news. The black, bearded screw, Mr
Armstrong, told me about it on the way over.

'You're sharing with a new lad, Lee; name of
Meaney. Usual overcrowding, I'm afraid. You bad
lads keep coming in.'

The new con was sitting on the top bunk
shovelling cornflakes in his face. Weird looking.
Very pale. No hair. His head looked like a light
bulb. With the light off.

I said, 'You can get down from there. New
cons go on the bottom.'

'Who said I were new?'

'The screw.'

'What does that black ★★★★★★ know, about anything?'

The great black take-over. That was his subject and he was worse than Stubby on digitalization. It was a relief when the door opened and a screw, not the same one, took me to classes.

Before he closed the door I said, 'By the way, Meaney, the last con to sleep in the top bunk was a big black Jamaican and a bed wetter.'

Result. By the time I got back he'd moved down and by going to classes I'd earned enough points to go to the gym that night.

But it would have been better if I hadn't.

The gym looked full when I got there. As always. It was one of – no, it were the *only* popular place inside. Except for the health centre.

The punch bags were taken mostly by black cons who looked like they were training for the Olympics. All the exercise bikes and rowing machines and weight-lifting gear were taken too.

'Come on, lad. Nothing doing here.' The screw was about to take me back to the cell, when there was a shout from the other side of the room.

'Lee, man! Over here!' Errol was on one of

the bikes, pointing to the empty running machine beside it.

I hadn't seen him since he punched Craig.

As I started running, he went off on one of his wheezy giggles.

'You trying to build up muscle, innit? Taking Errol's advice?'

I never did know what to make of him. One minute he was high as a kite, your best mate. Next, he was at your throat. I suppose it depended on what he was on. Or how much he was getting. Or what he wanted. Right now he looked like he was on steroids, leaning back, flexing his biceps, which popped up like buns in a toaster.

'Your old lady coming to see you soon, yeah? And that little girl with the bouncy boobs?'

It were a sore point. Excuse the pun. I hadn't heard from Kirstie for weeks and she didn't answer my calls. Not that I'd been able to ring her on Rule 49.

'She not getting it from some other fella, innit?'

It weren't something I liked to think about.

'You better giving your card to me, not wasting good money on her.'

I wished he'd keep his voice down. Mr

Skinner, the ponytailed screw, the one Sharpey said was bent, had just come in with Craig and Scab Face. And Sharpey.

Sharpey in the gym?

What was this? He never came here.

The three of them just stood there, like skittles in a row, while the screw went to talk to Mr O'Malley the instructor.

Something was up. I sensed it even before Craig nodded, sort of in my direction. It was hard to tell with One-eye.

Anyway, Scab Face strolled over and the con on the bike beside me got off. Scab Face got on the bike but didn't start pedalling.

Craig just stood there by the door staring with his one eye.

What was this about?

Errol seemed unaware. Was still going on about my phone card. 'You wouldn't give it to some other con, would you, Lee man?'

'Course not.'

I dunno if Mr O'Malley, the instructor, sensed something was up, but he came over soon after to record our scores.

'Good lad, Lee. You're working really hard. We'll start you at a higher level next time.'

Scab Face started pedalling.

'Well done, Jason. You're making progress. See what exercise and staying off the booze will do.'

Jason? It took me a second to realize he meant Scab Face.

Then the instructor turned his attention to the two by the door.

'You.' He obviously didn't know Sharpey. 'The rowing machine will be free shortly. Go stand by it. Craig,' he looked at his watch, 'Errol will be off the bike soon.'

Mr O'Malley headed off after Sharpey, thinking he'd defused any trouble.

Wrong.

Errol laughed. He had no intention of making way for Craig. And he hadn't finished with me.

'Higher level, man.' Reaching out, he pressed the button that increased the speed on my machine.

I went for the decrease but he flicked my hand away.

'Thought you was taking my advice, man. Building up your stamina, innit.'

I began to puff a bit.

Craig strolled over.

Errol laughed again. 'If you ain't got a card, what else you got, man?'

Craig and Scab Face heard him. I knew they did. But I don't think that was the trigger. They had it in for me before that. From the moment they came into the room with Sharpey. What happened next was planned before this. I'm not sure if Errol was part of the plan, or if what he was doing just happened to suit it.

'What else you got, innit, man?' Craig did a bad imitation of Errol's gravelly voice.

I didn't answer. It was all I could do to stop myself going arse over tit.

My heart was pounding.

Scab Face got off his bike and moved closer. Craig moved closer too. 'We all know Leesie here's a two-timer, but did you know he was a grass as well?'

'Grass,' hissed Scab Face as he pressed the increase.

'Grass.' No more than a whisper but it carried.

I sensed movement. Errol getting off his bike? I weren't sure. I was wondering how to make a quick exit.

Jump?

Off a running belt?

Not with Craig and Scab Face so close. Too close.

'Sings like a birdie,' said Craig.

'Sings like a birdie,' Scab Face echoed and pressed the increase. 'To the screws' tune.'

Sweat was dripping in front of my eyes, but I sensed people gathering.

'Grass.' The word had gone round.

No one likes a grass.

I could hardly see. Hardly breathe. I was gasping. Had a jabbing pain in my side. Feet going like the clappers.

'Grass.' A white hand flashed in front of me. The belt beneath my feet went faster. It was like running on ice. But my feet felt like fire.

'Grass.' A black hand hit the increase. Taunting me.

'Grass! Grass! Grass! Grass!'

'Fast! Fast!'

'Fast! Fast!'

Everyone was at it. A storm of whispers. Couldn't the screws hear? Couldn't they see?

'Grass! Grass! Grass! Grass!'

'Grass! Grass! Grass! Grass!'

I felt bodies crowding in.

Saw a blur of faces.

Smelled sweat and hatred.

But one face stood out. A ferrety face with a grin.

Sharpey's. By the door.

He'd set this up. He'd lied about me.

This was his revenge for me hitting him.

I wanted to shout 'Lying s—'

But it was too late. My legs were buckling. I felt my face hit the belt then pain as if my skin were being scraped by red hot sandpaper.

CHAPTER 20

Bastards. They got away with it.

Mr O'Malley said I'd overexerted myself.

The only good result was that I got a couple of days in sickbay. Not that sharing with a new con on detox was great. His screaming kept me awake on the first night, and on the second, one of the dafter window warriors joined in. Face like raw meat he had. The other cons had given him a kicking for keeping them awake.

I looked like I belonged to some primitive tribe. Sister Rogers showed me in a mirror. 'Well, nobody can call you a malingerer, can they?'

I had this big red stripe down the middle of my face. The belt had taken half my nose off.

She said she spent a lot of her time turning away fakers who fancied a few days off the wing. Why hadn't I thought of that?

It was good looking out of the window at the falling leaves and squirrels darting about. I know, I know. You think leaves and squirrels are nothing to get excited about. But most likely you haven't been locked up in a cell for days on end with nothing to look at but tarmac or concrete.

I asked Sister Rogers why the windows in the sickbay had bars. Couldn't imagine anyone wanting to break out. She said they were to stop cons breaking in.

'For the drugs. But the new governor wants to get rid of them,' she said. 'The bars not the drugs.'

'New governor?' First I'd heard of it.

She said they'd only had an acting governor for months. That's why things had been a bit chaotic. Or topsy-turvy as Mr McGiven called it. But the new permanent one, Mr Thompson, wanted to introduce some changes.

'Like what?'

'Eating together. Dining out, he calls it. To help with your rehab.'

'How?'

'By making inside more like outside. Get you used to sitting round a table and eating with other people like at home. Making conversation. Don't rate his chances, though. It'll make extra work for the officers.'

Nor did I and I didn't see the point. Most people eat in front of the TV.

While I was there I got a letter from Ken Lewis, the geezer who shopped me, saying he was coming to the next visiting. I'd filled in one of my Visiting Orders for him. It seemed a good idea at the time – anything to break the boredom – but did I really want to see him?

Anyway, on the following Wednesday – I was back on the wing by then – he was one of the first to arrive in the classroom set up for visiting.

'What you got hidden in your beard, Grandad?' The other cons had a go as he walked in. 'Search it, did they?'

'Is that a beer belly or have you got a bird under there?'

Ken – I'll give him that – handled it well. He laughed and said, 'Hi, you guys' in that sing-song voice of his – I think he was Welsh – as if he'd just walked into the community centre. He was the manager of the one on the estate and acted as if he owned it. Anyway, as soon as he sat down he said he'd brought me some 'treats' and a couple of letters. One from my mum. They were being vetted though.

Bastard. The sight of him brought it all flooding back.

He said, 'Your mum's got some news for you.'

'News? What's up?'

He stroked his beard.

My guts started churning. I didn't want to talk to him, but I had to know. 'Mick hasn't been at her, has he?'

'No no. Nothing like that. She was fine when I picked up the letter.'

'What then?'

He sucked in his bottom lip. 'She's gone to Spain, Lee. Her brother sent her the ticket, so she could go and work for him.'

'Work for him?' I was sounding like a parrot.

'Yes.'

It took a while for that to sink in.

'So she'll have to live there?'

He nodded. 'She'd had enough, Lee. She was behind with the rent, hadn't got a job, so she did a flit. For a fresh start.'

'In Spain?'

He tried to get me to talk about other things. The courses I was doing. The food. The case coming up. What I'd done to my face. But I couldn't concentrate. My mum had left me!

Ken ran his hands through his hair. 'I know how you feel, Lee, but try and see it from her point of view.'

Hers? But Mum and me, we'd always stuck *together*. Always. I was doing my best in here for *her*. To put things right between us.

If she'd gone what was the point?

'Lee.' Ken touched my hand and tried to fix me with one of his stern looks. 'I *do* know what it's like in here.'

I glanced round – at Errol with his dad, and Sharpey with his sister and Stumpy crying his eyes out because his visitors were leaving, and the screws watching and listening to everything.

I said, 'You haven't a clue. Nobody don't who's never been inside.'

'Who says I've never been inside?'

'I don't mean visiting.'

'Nor do I. Nor do I. Look at me.' He snapped. 'Look at me, Lee. *Nor do I.*'

I looked. What was he getting at? He looked

dead serious. His eyes were looking straight into mine. Did he mean what I thought he meant?

'You? Inside?'

He nodded. 'Yes, I'm an old lag, Lee.'

He laughed at my face. 'Close your mouth, lad. There's a fly buzzing round in here.'

'You're having me on. What d'y'do?'

'Thieving. Same as you. I was young and stupid once. But now I'm a pillow of the community as Mrs Haggerty says. Well, of the community centre. Pissy little job you once called it. Well, it might not seem much to you, but . . .'

'Sorry . . .'

He waved away my apology. 'Think what you like, lad, but I'm proud of myself, actually. I do a useful job. I pay my way. I support a wife and family. What I'm trying to say, Lee, is that *you* can turn yourself round. I think we write our own life stories, see. All right, maybe we can't choose the beginning and ending, but we can choose the middle. You can *choose* to spend your life in places like this, or you can *choose* to have a decent life outside. I once said you were your own jailer. Remember? No I don't suppose you do, so I'll say it again. *You put yourself inside.*'

'You helped.'

'Yes, I shopped you, and I'm not sorry. It was the right thing to do, but you committed the crime.'

The room had gone silent. When he stopped one of the cons clapped and shouted, 'Another cuppa tea, vicar?'

At least he lowered his voice for the rest of it.

'You did it, Lee, and you're paying for it.'

'That case hasn't even come up yet.'

'Well, I hope it goes well with you.'

'Hypocrite. You'll be giving evidence against me.'

'I am not a hypocrite. I do hope it goes well for you, and it might if you can convince the court you've changed. If you're keeping out of trouble. Are you?' His eyes held mine.

'It ain't that easy.'

'I know, but you do have a choice, Lee. You can come out of here a better person or a better criminal. You get lessons for both in here.'

He looked at his watch and got up. 'Sorry, but I've got a train to catch. You're a bright lad.

There are opportunities inside. Don't throw them away.'

When I got back to the cell there was a note to say I could collect my visitor's gifts from Reception and my letters. Ken had brought chocolate and deodorant and decent toothpaste.

He *did* know about inside.

I took it all back to my cell. Climbed onto the top bunk to get as far as I could from Meaney to read the letters. One in a pink envelope had Kirstie's writing on it, but I thought I'd get the bad news over first.

Dear Lee,

By the time you get this I will be in Spain. Bob's got me a job cleaning the villas' before they go on sale. Sorry but hitting me was the final straw. It was your dad all over again. They say criminals have an extra cromsome or something. Jeans, and I'm starting to think there rite. Anyway the doctor says Ive got to look out for myself now and get my nerves sorted out,

Mum

Great. No hope then.

I was doomed to be like my old man.

'Oh dear.' Light Bulb stood reading over my shoulder. 'I hope the other one's better.'

CHAPTER 21

Dear Lee

Sorry I haven't been in touch for a while, but I've been doing a lot of overtime and I've been thinking a lot. And I don't know how to say this really, not without hurting you . . .

I should have stopped reading there.

but I don't think you and me have got a future together. I just don't think you're the One For Me.

That's when I chucked it on the floor. Mistake.

Light Bulb picked it up and read it out in a daft high voice.

'Thing is, Lee, I've been talking to your mum and hearing about your dad and how violent you can be has made me scared. I've heard about men like that and well . . . as your mum says a lepard don't change its spots . . .'

'Nah, it's because you aren't big enough for her, Leesie!'

You could tell who he was in with.

'She's gone for someone more like me!' He grabbed his dick and started thrusting at the wall. 'Uh. Uh. Uh.'

Then he changed places and did the daft voice again.

'Oooooooooh! Ooooooh! Aaaaaah! That's better, Meaney.'

I said, 'It's no big deal.'

But I was filling up. It was taking everything I'd got to hold myself together. When the screw came to take us to hotplate I said I weren't hungry because I had a gut ache. Then, at last, when he'd hustled Meaney out and I were on my own, I let go.

I punched the wall till my fist bled.

And blubbed my guts out.

'Some of this help?' Stumpy put his head round the door later. I was curled up on the top bunk and hadn't seen him coming.

Open Door. That was one of the new governor's innovations. For half an hour after hotplate. Not that we could wander far, only on the spur. The rule was we had to ask before going into each other's cells. You can guess how many stuck to that.

I was glad it were Stumpy and none of the others.

Bet Meaney was telling them all about Kirstie.

They'd all been dead jealous ever since they'd seen her. Now they'd be gloating.

Who had sent Stumpy? The muppet didn't even keep his voice down and he had a spliff in his hand. I told him to come in and close the door because there were still screws about.

Mind you, it was a pair who liked a quiet life, so we were probably safe enough.

I told Stumpy to sit down on the karzy or the bottom bunk. But that confused him. A choice.

So I said, 'Sit on the bottom bunk, Stumpy. Meaney, the new cons, with Craig and Scab Face.'

Those three were thick as thieves.

Clichés. We'd just done them in English. Can't see what's wrong with them myself. They were thick and they were thieves.

Stumpy said, 'Thank you, Lee,' in that slow way of his.

Was being a criminal in Stumpy's genes? Doing what he was told was, and that amounted to the same thing if you lived where Stumpy lived. If you had so-called mates like Stumpy's. They got him to do their dirty work for them.

'See that DVD, Stumpy. Go get it for me.'

'See that big guy, Stumpy. He's bad. Go thump him.'

And it was as bad in here. Stumpy were a comic turn.

'Go ask that con why his old lady don't like dancing, Stumpy. Go on. That one.'

Off Stumpy went.

'Why don't your old lady like dancing?'

Everybody heard him asking, and everybody fell about when the con's fist came out and hit Stumpy in the face. They all knew the con's mum didn't have any legs, see.

I said, 'Who sent you, Stumpy?'

'Errol.'

That figured. He was back on the spur. Errol had been in visiting with his old man. Delivery day. So he'd seen me and knew I had stuff to trade. But he didn't have what I needed. I felt like getting bladdered. But the spliff would have to do. I thanked Stumpy and told him to go and tell Errol I'd pay him later.

Your dad all over again.

I couldn't get the words of Mum's letter out of my head.

Ken had said, 'Try and see it from her point of view.' They all said that. 'Feel your victim's pain.'

But Mum weren't in pain. She was sunbathing in Spain. She hadn't listened to a word I said about making it up to her and going straight.

And pigs might fly, Lee.

And she'd told Kirstie. And Kirstie believed her.

Though I'd never hit her.

I drew on the spliff, but it didn't stop me thinking about my old man. Why was I following in his footsteps when I didn't want to be? Was I programmed like a robot? Was it in the genes?

Didn't wanting to be different count for anything?

Hadn't I *learned* to be a tea leaf from the one who'd got me to climb through windows for him? Because it were good fun. All those sweets, and later, pocket money for helping. And Mum didn't ask too many questions about where I got it.

Don't blame other people. Take responsibility.

The door opened again. 'Didn't think you did this stuff, Leesie.'

The air was pretty thick by now.

Sharpey perched himself on the bog, ignoring Stumpy. 'Heard you had a visitor this afternoon.'

I didn't answer.

'Ken from the estate. Just hope you didn't say anything silly.'

Didn't need to ask who he'd been talking to.

I said, 'You think Ken doesn't know about Mick?'

'Hope he don't go dropping him in it then. Wouldn't like anything to happen to Ken, or his nice community centre. It would be terrible if it burned down or something. How's your mum?'

While he was talking I started to feel a bit

mellow and a better thought drifted in. If Mum
was in Spain, Mick couldn't get to her. I didn't
have to worry about her getting done over. She
were safe at least.

'Craig says . . .'

I flapped my arms and squawked. 'You his
parrot now?'

'Well, if you don't wanna know.'

'I don't.'

Mick could still get me of course, when I got
out. But I could look after myself. So could Ken.
He knew a thing or two, he did.

But 'outside' still seemed like a distant planet.
What if I did get there and Mick was there
waiting? Offering me the sort of job opportunities that would put me back inside?

Do a job for me, Lee, and I'll leave you alone.

If Mum were right I'd accept. If it were in
the genes. If I were programmed like a Dalek.

'I-am-a-crim-in-al-and-I-will-do-any-thing-
you-ask.'

Sharpey said, 'You OK, Leesie?' He was
standing by the bunk now. I'd forgotten he was
there.

I said, 'Sharpey, you're a shit, I'm a shit and
life's shit. There's no hope.'

He laughed. 'I told you you'd need this, sooner or later.'

He was waving his toothbrush.

'What for, slit my wrists?'

'Not yet, Leesie. You've got something else to do first. The job. It's tonight.'

'Job?'

'Craig's job. He says tonight's our best chance with Skinno on duty.'

I said, 'Go drop one, Sharpey. Tell 'em all to drop one.'

He said, 'Haven't you learned nothing? You'll regret this if you don't. Look, I'm leaving this here. Take care of it and be ready when Cheesey comes.'

Well, that's what I thought he said. But I didn't care. The ceiling light was flying towards me.

CHAPTER 22

Errol came into the cell later.

Like a great black cloud. At first I thought he was in a mood because Stumpy had come back without getting paid. So, as he slumped onto the karzy, spliff in mouth, I said, 'I've got chocolate or shower gel. I told Stumpy.'

But he just sat there.

Smoke was seeping under the door onto the landing. On any other night the screws would have been rushing around like the fire brigade.

He mumbled something.

'What was that?' I moved to the bottom of the bunk to hear better.

''S my little girl.'

'Amy-Jane?'

Wrecked as I was, I could see this was serious. His eyes were bloodshot like one of those big dogs with barrels of brandy round their necks. But say the wrong thing and his hands could be round my throat.

'What's up, man?' It was the best I could do.

His little girl was very ill. She'd got a rare virus. It was touch and go. She was in hospital. Intensive care.

'I wanna go and see her, man. Real bad I do. The guvnor, he say I can, but then my old lady ring him and say "*No way*". She say, "*Don' let him out. Don' let him come and see his little girl.*"'

'Why not?'

He just drew on the spliff.

It was weird. I thought he'd be going ape shit, breaking things up. Going for someone's throat. That's what he usually did if you stopped him doing what he wanted to do. But he weren't mad. He was gutted. He had a photo in one hand and I guessed who it was.

'Why don't she want you to see her, man?'

He mumbled something. There was 'hit' in there somewhere.

'You hit her? Your old lady?'

'So she scared of seeing me, innit?' He stared at the floor as if he wanted to disappear into it.

I knew how he felt. Like a slug. But there aren't really words – well I can't think of them – to describe exactly how you feel. I just know that sometimes I'd like to crawl out of my own skin.

Leave myself behind.

I said, 'Know how you feel, man. My mum's the same. She don't want to see me no more. Says I'll do it again. Like my old man.'

'You hit your old lady?'

I nodded.

And she's told Kirstie.

I couldn't say that.

'The sins of the fathers.' He drew on the spliff. 'That what she say. Will be visited upon the children. From generation to generation, innit?'

His hands were together and I wondered if he was saying his prayers. Wondered if I should press the cell bell and ask for the chaplain. It were getting dark outside and I felt myself being dragged down into whatever black pit he was in.

'We're cursed, man.'

Then what hope was there of going straight?

Hope is a good thing and good things never die.
But what good had I ever done?

'Doctors,' I said. 'They do wonders these days. Amy-Jane. She'll be all right.'

But he seemed to have forgotten I was there. And I was floating to the ceiling again now.

Then we heard a scream.

Alarm bells started ringing. Really. At first it sounded as if they were in the distance. Then they seemed louder and we realized screws were rushing about banging doors. But before they got to us, we got up and wandered out onto the landing to look over the rail into Association below.

Where someone was screaming. Writhing on the floor. Screams were echoing all round the building.

It was Wayne – tattoo head – we learned later. The con who'd come in the same day as me, along with Harley. He'd beaten Craig at pool and said something about it not being hard, beating a one-eyed con. Joking like. But Craig didn't see the joke. He picked up the cue and poked Wayne's eye out.

Right out.

Well, the screws moved in and carted him off.

So he wasn't going to be adjusting anyone's car tonight. I was off that hook. And for a bit I felt better.

But there was still Kirstie's letter.

. . . a lepard don't change its spots . . .

CHAPTER 23

Errol perked up.

He said the new guvnor was very supportive and allowed him to ring the hospital to ask about Amy-Jane. And they said she was hanging on and was a real little fighter.

I got a phone call too. At first I hoped it was Kirstie to say she'd changed her mind. But it was Ken. He must have rung up and arranged it with the screws, because one of them took me down to Sosh to get it. He ummed and ahed a bit – and I could imagine him pulling on his beard – then said there was something he'd forgotten to say.

'I just want you to know, Lee, that if you

decide to go straight, I'll be there for you when you get out. You won't be on your own, lad.'

Well, I started to fill up. Most people are just out for themselves.

'And I believe you can do it, if you make up your mind.'

Shut up, Ken. Other cons were watching.

I suppose he knew the screws were listening in, because he didn't say any more. Didn't *say* that he'd managed to change, turn himself round, and that if he had I could, but the words were sort of there. I managed to thank him for the stuff he'd brought in.

'And everything.'

I was still gutted about Kirstie's letter, but a walk in the park helped.

That came about because Errol started going to chapel, and the chapel was a room in the health centre. Errol wanted to pray for Amy-Jane and he asked some of us to go with him. Well, I had to put in a Special Request, but it was granted. There were four of us – plus screw – Harley, Stumpy, me and Errol.

I were surprised there weren't more, but perhaps he hadn't asked more.

Anyway, we were like kids when we got to the park, kicking the leaves and picking up conkers and throwing them at each other. But the screw made us put them down before we went in.

Dangerous weapons, see.

Leroy and Winston were already there, helping the chaplain with candles and things. She was one of these lady vicars, dressed in black with a white collar. But the chapel was colourful. There was a blue carpet on the floor and white flowers with a heady smell and orange chairs to sit on and rainbow-striped cushions to kneel on. Cool. The chaplain went on a bit, but as far as I was concerned she could have gone on as long as she liked. If it did the business for Amy-Jane, it was fine by me. And it was good singing 'All Things Bright and Beautiful'.

And we were off the wing.

Things there went on much as before despite the new governor's so-called innovations. Body searches. Room searches. At different times each day so you never knew when they were coming. Screws still read your letters and listened to your calls. You still spent hours thinking about stuff you'd rather not think about.

The biggest change was 'dining out'.

Which proved to be a big mistake.

First the kitchen in C-wing was brought back into service, though only on two nights a week. It was alongside the Association area, which became a dining room. There was a serving hatch between the two. Some cons got jobs helping prepare food, so it was dead popular with them, and with most of us.

But not the screws.

We got to eat thirty at a time so there were five tables, six of us at each. Quite close together, though the pool table had been removed after the eye-poking incident. Out of Parkhall and all the YOIs, so someone said. Cues were reclassi-fied as dangerous weapons and the government banned them.

Anyway, you could tell the screws didn't like it – dining out, I mean. They issued dire warn-ings about it being a privilege that could be withdrawn at any time. There was plenty of scope for trouble. Boiling water. Knives. Cons in close contact.

But it went all right the first time.

And the second.

It went all right till the day Amy-Jane died.

Yes, she died, despite all the prayers and hymns and being a little fighter.

Errol was gutted, even before he got the letter from his old lady saying she didn't want him at the funeral. But that really did for him. She said it was all the dirt and the filth and sin inside that killed Amy-Jane. She must have caught the virus when she was visiting the prison.

In other words, she blamed Errol.

Well, he went into a dark pit where no one could reach him. His personal officer tried. The medics tried with antidepressants and stuff. The chaplain tried. She offered to hold a sort of funeral for Amy-Jane. Called it a memorial service. She said she'd say prayers and stuff and we'd sing hymns and remember the good things about the little girl. She got a group of us together to talk about it. She asked us to persuade Errol. Said it would do him good.

But Errol wouldn't listen. He wouldn't come out of his cell.

I went to see him during Open Door, found him sitting on his bunk with his head in his hands. I went in and said I thought the service would be a good idea, and the walk through the park would be nice. But he just shook his rasta head and said he wanted a proper funeral, where he could see Amy-Jane and say sorry and goodbye.

'Course you do.'

I turned and saw Sharpey standing in the doorway.

'Course you do,' he said again, shaking his head, all understanding like. 'You want a proper funeral. It's only right.'

I should have taken more notice. I should have watched that rodent's every move.

But I didn't and I didn't realize that Errol was a ticking bomb.

Or that certain forms of low life were getting ready to light the fuse.

CHAPTER 24

On the day of Amy-Jane's funeral – it was a Friday – I was surprised to see Errol in the so-called dining room because he hadn't been out of his room for days. He was sitting by himself, with his head in his hands at a table near the back. The screws were in place round the sides. Four of them. I queued at the serving hatch, got my grub and went and sat by him.

He hadn't got any grub so I said, 'Aren't you eating?'

He didn't answer and another con sat down at the other side.

The other tables were filling up.

I said, 'If you don't get something soon, there'll be nothing left.'

But it was as if I hadn't spoken. As if I wasn't there. He took no notice. Nor did any of the screws.

Then Craig and Scab Face walked in. Followed by Meaney and Stumpy. And Sharpey brought up the rear. Nothing unusual in that, except that One-eye hadn't been around for a bit.

I assumed a screw had brought them down from the landing. I didn't give a second glance.

Till I noticed the humming. And I didn't notice that till they were standing in front of our table. Then I recognized the tune.

'Der dum di der.

Der der dumdi dumdi der.'

The Funeral March.

I'll never know why the screws didn't stop it right then. Perhaps they didn't see or hear. It weren't loud exactly. Perhaps they saw but wanted something to go wrong so they had a reason to withdraw the privilege. Or perhaps they were stunned.

Like I was.

I didn't do anything either. Didn't know what

to do. I was frozen to the seat. Mesmerized. Dumb. Unbelieving.

'Der dum di der.

Der der dumdi dumdi der.'

They were carrying something, though they kept it low and hidden. It weren't till they got real close that I saw it was a small white box, and you didn't need to be a genius to guess what it were supposed to be.

I felt sick. And scared. And full of foreboding.

'Der dum di der.

Der der dumdi dumdi der.'

Errol still had his head in his hands. Didn't seem to see or hear.

But I couldn't be sure. Couldn't see his eyes. Didn't know if they were open or closed.

'Errol, mate.' Craig was the spokesman, using that soft slow voice of his. 'We're sorry you couldn't go to your little girl's funeral.'

'Sorry,' echoed Scab Face.

'So,' Craig nodded at the others and they lowered the box onto the table. 'We thought we'd bring the funeral to you.'

It had a cross and RIP on it and a bunch of yellow flowers. I dread to think what was inside.

I held my breath.

Errol still seemed as if he hadn't seen it. That was one good thing. The other was that the screws caught on at last. I could hear one behind me on his radio saying to send reinforcements pronto because trouble was brewing. I wanted to do something, but didn't know what.

Come on, Errol, let's get out of here.

The words were in my mouth. I wanted to take hold of his arm and lead him away, out of the door behind us. Well, part of me did. The other part was scared to touch him. Scared to break the trance he seemed to be in. Maybe he hadn't seen or heard, I thought hopefully.

Or maybe all these thoughts came later. Afterwards. Too late.

Frozen to the spot. That's what I was. Everyone was. Except Craig. He was lowering himself into a crouching position, opposite Errol, so their faces were level.

'Look, mate. Daddy, we're doing a funeral for you.'

'F-f-funeral,' said Scab Face.

Someone shouted, 'Open the box!' Someone else laughed.

There was another 'Open the box!'

And Errol looked up.

'Don't you want to say goodbye?' said Craig.

And at that moment I hated them, all of them. Errol was dying inside and they were baiting him like a bear on a chain. But they'd forgotten something.

Errol wasn't on a chain.

CHAPTER 25

It was so quiet you could have heard a feather drop.

Errol didn't answer. He just looked at One-eye still crouching opposite. Face to face they were, about two foot between them.

No one said anything.

No one did anything.

Then a screw's radio crackled and it sounded like thunder.

The screws were stirring, starting to do something at last. But the other cons took no notice. Least of all Errol. I could feel the heat of his body beside me, hear his breath going in and out, see the knotted veins in his neck, and a pulse throbbing. I smelled sweat and rage.

And hatred.

He'd seen and heard. Everything. Suddenly I knew he had, even before he turned towards me.

'Get you later, man.'

I'll never forget his bloodshot eyes smouldering. My mouth went dry. Did he think I had something to do with it? That I'd set it up? I remembered Sharpey standing by me talking about a 'proper funeral'. Where *was* Sharpey?

There at the back, watching, and something told me this was his idea.

Errol turned back to Craig. I opened my mouth to say 'Not me,' but he weren't listening.

Craig was still gripping the edge of the table, face between his fists, looking at Errol with his one bullet-grey eye.

And Errol looked straight back at him, hands flat on the table now. I heard him take a breath and thought he was going to say something. The screws moved in but they were too late.

Errol lunged forward, arms outstretched. Then his huge hands grasped Craig's neck.

Squ . . . eeeeeeee . . . zing.

All I could see was Craig's open mouth and a yellowy brown tongue sticking out of it, gasping. And his arms at the side flapping. Then there was a crack as his head fell back and a wet gurgling sound.

It took all four screws to prise Errol's hands from round Craig's neck, and pull him off. But they couldn't hold him. And it was too late for One-eye. Limp, he flopped forward. Then, when Errol jerked the table upwards, the body flipped backwards.

Now Errol grabbed the table with both hands and held it above his head. Lurching this way and that, he roared like a hunted animal that wasn't going down without a fight.

Was he looking for me?

Was it my turn next?

I looked for somewhere to hide.

Get you later, man. His words were in my ears.

I moved back when the table went flying, and found myself flat against the back wall. Behind him, but still in his reach if he turned. There was a door on my left but it was shut, and I didn't know where it went. Or what it was. A cupboard?

An exit? Where to? And it was most likely locked. But I edged sideways towards it.

'RIOT!'

I don't know who yelled that but suddenly everyone was at it. There were tables and chairs and food and dishes and knives and forks flying everywhere. And fists. Was it one gang against another? Cons against screws? There was no way of telling. It looked like a free-for-all. I lost track of who was where. I lost track of Errol, though I was trying to keep my eye on him.

'Get you later, man.'

A lot of old scores were settled that night. And the screws didn't hang around to see. There were a few shouts of 'Back to your places!' and 'Sit down!' Two of them tried to pull down the metal screen between the kitchen and the serving hatch. But they were stopped by cons climbing over the counter into the kitchen.

Errol, was he one of them?

It was then that the screws scarpered. Must have been the thought of all the knives in there. They ran out, slamming doors behind them.

Then Sharpey was standing on a table, shouting.

'Build barricades in front of the doors! The screws'll be back and we'll be ready for 'em!'

But most of them took no notice. They were too busy fighting each other.

Then Sharpey grabbed Meaney. I don't know what Light Bulb said but Sharpey punched him in the gut. Meaney clutched his side. Crumpled.

I saw the knife in Sharpey's hand. He was wiping the blade on his pants. And he saw me watching. Knew that I'd seen.

'Listen to me, you *******.' All eyes turned towards him. 'Break down that door!' He pointed to the door behind me. 'Break that down! Then up the stairs to the roof!'

And I'd thought he was a backroom boy. A shifty little sewer rat.

'You . . .' He jabbed his finger at me. 'You do your bit!'

By now alarm bells were ringing. And the fire sprinklers were going. Raining down. And some cons were panicking. Didn't know what to do.

So Sharpey told them. Again. 'Break down the effing door!'

Some rushed for it. Started ramming it with their shoulders. Again and again they went at it. Uselessly. Senselessly.

It must have been painful but they didn't feel

it. On a surge of adrenalin they went at it again and again and it still didn't budge.

Sharpey shouted into the kitchen. 'Get something to get the hinges off!'

I caught sight of Stumpy sitting under the counter banging his head on the floor. Then two cons scrambled over him, one with a knife, one with a cleaver like a machete. Others followed waving saucepans and trays and big soup ladles. Funny? No.

'Out of the way! Let us through!'

The shoulder bangers stepped back as the cons with knives headed for the door by me. They started hacking round the hinges. First the con with the cleaver got one off. Then he started hacking at another.

'Out of the way!' The door crashed to the floor.

A cheer went up.

Then Sharpey was shouting again. 'Through the door! To the roof!'

And now they all did as he said. There was a stampede through the door. Shouts and yells.

I went too. Was swept off my feet. Saw stairs in front of me. Rampaged up them. So did everyone.

But a hiding place was what I wanted. I just wanted to lie low till it was all over. Keep out of everyone's way. But as the rest of them stormed up the stairs, I had to go with them. They were a tide carrying me along. I was in the middle of a mad howling screaming surging tide.

I had no choice.

There I go again. But it had never been truer. I was trapped.

Till I tripped.

Felt myself falling forward. For a bit I was still carried upwards. Then I started sliding down. It went black. I heard the mob baying. Felt them trampling over me. On and on pounding my body. Smashing my face against the steps.

Then it stopped.

For a second I lay there listening. Then I let myself slide to the bottom of the stairs.

And I saw Sharpey in the dark space under the stairs. Crouched in the corner.

With a knife.

CHAPTER 26

I lay still. Hoped he'd think I was dead. Kept my eyes shut. Almost.

Could see the knife glinting in his hand. A kitchen knife. Blade six inches long.

The light was behind me. It came from the dining area and lit him. Put me in shadow. Good.

He was crouching knife in hand. Ready to spring.

Sharpey. Start a riot and disappear. That figured. Get the others going, then vanish. Wait for the screws. Say he'd had nothing to do with it. Now he just wanted to save his skin.

So did I.

But I knew what he'd done to Meaney, and he knew that I knew.

He knew I could tell the screws, if he didn't stop me. I saw him peering, trying to figure if I was dead. If I weren't he'd finish me off. He had nothing to lose. And lots to gain.

He said, 'You get up on the roof with the others, Leesie.'

I stayed dead.

He said, 'You go and stand by your mates.'

I stayed dead.

'If you're man enough, woman slapper.'

He wanted to be alone when the screws came. Looking innocent. As if butter wouldn't melt.

I still stayed dead, though I felt fear and rage rising. Felt the blood pumping through me. Felt myself take a breath.

And he saw it. Or heard it. I saw his face twitch. Saw him think he'd got to investigate. Saw him getting to his feet, left hand levering himself up. Right hand on the knife.

And I moved. Before he was upright.

I sprang forward. Headfirst. Into his crutch. Felt my head smash into his balls. Heard him yell. Saw the knife drop.

I grabbed it and felt the fire in my blood.

Now we faced each other but I had the knife. And his balls were hurting. He was whimpering.

I felt the hilt in my hand, fingered the blade. Sharp for Sharpey.

I'd never have a better chance. I could slit his throat.

'You wouldn't, Leesie.'

He looked up, fear in his eyes. I smelled piss. Saw it splattering the floor.

'Oh – yes – I – would. You deserve it, Sharpey, for all the times you've done this to other people. You deserve it for carrying out Mick's dirty work.'

And if I do you won't be able to do it any more.

I raised my hand.

And smelled shit. He was filling his pants. Crapping himself.

I stepped back.

The stink? Or the thought of spending the rest of my life inside because of him? I dunno.

But I stepped back.

Left him sobbing in his own crap.

CHAPTER 27

Where to go? That was the question.

Where to hide?

Word had got round. The building shook with all the chanting, stamping, pipe-banging, shouting, alarm ringing, siren blaring. The riot squad were on their way. Water was squirting from all directions.

Upstairs?

But not to the roof. Not with the others.

Halfway?

Yes, a landing. Doors without hatches.

I tried a handle. Tried another. Desperate now. The sirens sounded close.

Tried a third. It opened. Fell in and a light

came on. Cupboard. Full of towels and sheets. I crept into a corner, the door closed and the light went out.

Good.

I didn't mind the dark. Oblivion: that's what if felt like. Nothingness. Fine by me. Madness outside. I jammed my feet against the door. Felt it throbbing and the wall throbbing behind me.

Like an earthquake.

And I was in its epicentre.

Then I was sliding across the floor, knees under my chin.

The door was opening.

I looked up and froze. Errol was in the doorway and I knew he'd come to kill me.

Why not? He had nothing to lose. He thought I'd helped with that funeral. *As if I'd help Sharpey*.

He stared at me with crazed eyes. Stood there nearly filling the doorframe; beads of water on his rasta hair, glistening like a halo.

And I just sat there. I don't think I could have moved. My adrenalin was all used up. I'd had enough. Just wanted him to get it over with quickly.

I said, 'If you're gonna do it, do it, muppet.'

It weren't bravery. Cold sweat were pouring down my neck. All the strength was draining out of me. I felt weak at the knees, weak in the arms. Weak all over. Sick.

Even before I saw the toothbrush.

I'd wondered where that had gone ever since Sharpey had left it on my bed. Thought the screws must have picked it up. But Errol had. Now he held it in front of me, waving it from side to side like one of those timing thingies for music.

I couldn't stop looking at it. Was hypnotized I suppose.

To and fro.

To and fro.

Knew I had a knife somewhere. Not far away. On the floor beside me. But I couldn't move. Paralysed.

Left to right.

Left to right.

So this was it. The end of my story. Was I writing it or was Errol? More thoughts came into my head. Who would come to my funeral?

Would Mum bother to come back from Spain? Kirstie? Ken? I remembered his last words. *Look after yourself.* Ken, he knew what it was all about. I saw him in my mind's eyes, in his community centre by the fruit machine, trying to get me to play table tennis. Or a computer game. To keep me off the street.

Saw me and Mum in our grotty flat. The concrete walkways. The stairs smelling of piss. Me as a little kid nicking stuff. Me in court.

Me in here. Inside.

Was this my life passing before my eyes?

'Amy-Jane.'

His voice made me look at his face which was grey and flaky. Except for dark lines where tears were running down his cheeks.

I said, 'I didn't . . .' Because, whatever happened, I wanted him to know I'd had nothing, nothing at all, to do with all that coffin stuff. I said, 'I had nothing to do with it. It made me sick. It weren't right. It were cruel and heartless and . . .'

I couldn't finish. I am not a hero in the story of my life. I wish I were but I weren't.

'. . . wrong.' I got the word out.

Then I closed my eyes and waited.

And he stepped forward. I heard him. Felt him towering over me. Then he moved and I thought, *this is it*. Braced myself. Death by tooth-brush. How quick could that be?

But nothing happened.

Was he winding me up? Playing cat and mouse?

I sneaked a look.

Up. Down. He weren't there.

Then I saw him beside me, on the floor slumped forward, feet sticking out of the doorway. Mumbling.

'Nothing. Nothing to lose. Nothing can hurt me now. Amy-Jane. Nothing.' It didn't make sense. He was still holding the toothbrush, but loosely now, in his right hand, which was on the floor.

Close to me.

I thought of taking it. Thought of trying to find the knife. Thought again.

If he were determined to kill me he would do it, with or without the toothbrush. And it was best not to disturb him. Better to get out of his way. If I could.

Forwards or backwards? Out of the door? Or into the dark at the back of the cupboard?

I shifted slightly, away from him. He didn't seem to notice. Was still mumbling away.

'Tried, man . . . wanted . . .'

Well, yes. I knew how he felt, but I eased forward.

'I wanted to be a good dad, Lee.'

So he did know I was there.

I said, 'You wrote that story for her.' He'd written this story about a bird in a cage who wants to go and see his baby bird but he can't. All he can do is sing that he loves her. 'Pictures too.'

But he didn't answer.

I waited, hoping he was falling asleep.

Waited, hoping he was so full of dope he'd pass out.

Waited, hoping to save my own skin.

When he didn't stir I shuffled forward, towards the door. But as I started to move, his arm went up and a blade caught the light.

My hands went up, expecting the blow.

Waited.

Waited.

Curled up in a ball like a baby.

Waited.

Then I opened my eyes, and saw I was in the far corner as far away from him as I could get.

Survival instinct. It's stronger than you think. I must have flung myself there when I saw his arm move. But I wasn't that far from where he was sitting now, his arm like a split hose.

But spurting blood. Blood everywhere. On the piles of sheets and towels. On the floor and walls. On me. Warm and sticky on my face. Salty on my lips.

Blood.

Errol had slit his left arm from his elbow to his wrist in a long jagged line. The dark skin lay open, showing a double line of pink flesh and yellow fat and in the middle a severed artery still pulsing.

Blood still gushing out.

His grey tracksuit bottoms were soaked with blood and he sat watching the stains spread.

Calmly.

'I'm coming, Amy-Jane.'

I said, 'No . . .'

I wish I could say that I picked up the sheet and tried to stop the blood flowing. That I jumped to his rescue like a regular little First Aider. That I rushed for help. But I didn't.

I puked. Threw up. All over.

And he didn't want me to stop it. It was his choice and it was too late to change his mind. The spurts of blood got slower as life ebbed out of him. But it took a long time.

I'll never forget that.

When they, the screws, came – I don't know when it was – I was still huddled in the corner, shaking. I just let them take me away. I'm not a hero.

Never will be.

CHAPTER 28

A wasted life.

That's what I thought when I saw his coffin sliding away. Saw the curtains close on Errol's life.

Ashes to ashes.

That's what the pastor said. Pastor was what they called the chaplain who ran Errol's funeral. He was a young black man.

But Errol weren't ashes, not in the beginning. He was a baby, then a little boy, then a teenager and he could have grown into a man and been lots of things. But now he weren't going to be anything.

Except ashes.

Before the crematorium there'd been a service

in a brick church somewhere in London with singing and swaying and clapping and prayers and lots of people, mostly black, shouting 'Alleluia!' And the pastor told this story about an old geezer who had two sons, one good one bad. But the bad one became good in the end and he made his old dad so happy he had this big party and barbecued a calf.

But Errol's mum didn't look happy. She was crying her eyes out.

Mr McGiven said I'd have to talk to her. Oh yes, he was there too. They didn't let me out on my own. And I were in handcuffs, fastened at the back so it didn't look so obvious, but it made it harder to walk.

And they did let me wear my own clothes. So it was a second outing for the chinos and Marks and Sparks shirt. Mr McGiven and me we sat at the back, behind everyone. Errol's mum, I recognized her in her white robes, was at the front. Her shoulders were shaking.

When the coffin came in, carried by six big blokes in black coats, I got a whiff of the red and white flowers, lilies and roses I think, and it took me back to the chapel when Errol was alive and still full of hope.

But there was no hope for Amy-Jane now, except Heaven, if you believe that stuff.

At the end we went outside and joined this long line of people queuing to 'pay our respects' to Errol's mum. Mr McGiven said I had to say a few words. I said I didn't know what to say, and couldn't we just leave?

But he said, 'No' and 'Just say what you feel.'

I said, 'I feel rubbish.'

He said, 'Well, what do you think Errol would like you to say to her?'

So, when my turn came, I told her that Errol loved her and Amy-Jane, and he was really sorry that he hit her and made a mess of his life.

And when she said, 'Then why didn't he say sorry?' I tried to explain.

'Because to say sorry he'd have to admit to himself first what he'd done. And if he did that he'd have to admit to himself that he was a rubbishy sort of person. Bad. The pits.'

Well, it sort of rhymed with pits but I couldn't say that to her.

'And if he did – if he knew he were a bad person – he wouldn't be able to live with himself.'

Which he couldn't in the end.

She said, 'How do you know all this?'

I said, 'Because he told me – and I feel the same.'

Because I did.

If you don't talk about things you can pretend they never happened. Up to a point. While you can do things to take you mind off it. Or when you're out of your head with drugs or booze. When, one way or another, you're hiding from yourself. But you can't do that inside.

Well, I couldn't.

Being inside your own head is the worst bit. You see it all. You know what you are. There's no escape.

She said, 'You hit your mum?'

And when I nodded she said, 'Well, you just repent your sins and make sure you live the rest of your life decent like.'

She gave me one of Errol's rings. Well, Mr McGiven had to take it from her.

'Wear it,' she said. 'When you get out, and if ever you go to raise your hand in anger, think of Errol.'

I didn't ask about the sins of the fathers stuff.

CHAPTER 29

Mr McGiven and me talked about it on the way back. We were in a minibus looking like normal people.

Almost.

He were driving and he let me sit in the passenger seat. In cuffs, though. Regulations.

I asked about what Mum had said about genes and chromosomes and stuff. He said experts disagree about it. He called it the Nature/Nurture debate. Are we born good or bad? Or does our upbringing make us good or bad? People have been debating that for centuries.

'Nowadays, most experts think certain

personality types are more likely to commit crimes. People who don't think before they act for instance. Or people who are easily led.'

Point taken.

'But it's not the same as being programmed. It does make a difference how you're brought up. Whether you're taught right from wrong for instance, but also whether you *choose* to do right or wrong. People aren't Daleks.'

He said violent people learn to be violent, often from their parents. My old man hadn't set a brilliant example.

But I wondered if some people don't learn *not* to be violent. If you get my gist? Perhaps people are born violent, some of them anyway.

We watched this little kid – we were stuck at traffic lights – go ape shit when his mum wouldn't let him let go of her hand and cross the road by himself. He hurled himself at her, pummelling her with the fist he had free. Kicking out at her too. And when she picked him up and held him at arm's length his legs were still kicking the air.

I don't think anyone taught him that. It was the red rage. I knew how he felt. I've seen cons acting like that. Like big violent two-year-olds with big dangerous fists. Or weapons. I've been like that myself. But that kid weren't bad, not through and through. He just hadn't learned how to act.

Had I? That was the question.

Well, I didn't knife Sharpey, did I? When I had the chance. I could have, and part of me wanted to, but I didn't.

Good things never die.

I wished that journey could go on and on. It was great watching the countryside fly by. See the evening sky streaked blue and pink and gold. See a hot air balloon shaped like a purple pig floating over the bare trees.

And pigs might fly, Lee.

Well, they did sometimes.

I wished we weren't going back to Parkhall. I wished we were going miles away in the other direction. Miles away from my old life.

But we weren't. Well, I weren't. Not yet.

I don't need to tell you what it were like going back. The gates clanging shut, the razor wire on top of the never-ending walls. The grey buildings and the faces pressed to the barred windows. The routine rub down search. The grey tracksuit. The yelling and banging. The stink.

Nothing had changed, see.

Well not much, and not for the better. The screws had done some re-organizing after the riot. They split up all the cons. Moved us around. The usual game of musical cells.

All privileges had stopped.

Did I say all the cons? I don't mean that. All the cons weren't there. Sharpey had been moved to prison proper. The CCTV cameras had caught him starting the riot, so the screws saw what he was like at last.

I was moved to A-wing but it was no different from C-wing. Except that I was on Rule 49 again. For my own protection, Mr McGiven said, because I gave evidence against Sharpey. Told them what he'd done to Meaney, Light Bulb, who was still in hospital.

I owed Mr McGiven. He'd persuaded the governor to let me go to Errol's funeral. So I wrote the letter he wanted me to write to Mrs Brown.

I told her I was sorry and I meant it. I said I'd try to make things right and get her jewellery back.

I named Mick Donaghue. I dobbed him in.

Grassing isn't the worst crime. Sometimes it isn't a crime. But it's dangerous. There'll be trouble waiting for me when I get outside, but I'll have to deal with it. Mick will always have it in for me. So will Sharpey, though it will be a long time before *he's* on the street. They'll both want to get their revenge.

So will Craig. One-eye? You thought he was dead? So did I. So did he most like, but doctors, they can do wonders these days.

Those three might change. Turn into good guys.

As I said, pigs sometimes fly. But most cons inside change for the worse it seems to me. Most get A-levels in crime and then degrees. So I'll have to risk some of them coming after me. Because I don't want to spend my life inside. I don't want to spend a life running away from myself. I want to be able to look myself in the eye when I shave on a morning. I don't want a shitty, scummy grey little life.

I want a life full of colours.

I don't want a manky, clanging-in-my-ears sort of life.

I want to listen to my own music.

I want a girl of my own who isn't afraid of me.

Be like my old man?

I'd rather be dead.

UPDATE

Lee got a suspended sentence of twelve months for the burglary of Mrs Brown's house.

He was released on licence on 23rd April 2008, after serving nine months of his sentence.

He is living in a YMCA hostel.

He is doing a computer course at Ken Lewis's community centre.

He meets regularly with his Youth Offending Team worker.

He has a job with a delivery company and is learning to drive.

He has a new girlfriend called Nikki.

At the time of going to print he has not re-offended.

ACKNOWLEDGEMENTS

I am indebted to Julie Laslett and Caroline Webster of Dramatic Media who created the character of Lee for their film, *Young Offender*. Their film took Lee to the door of the cell to begin his sentence. My novel begins where their film ends. Julie Laslett listened to every word of an early draft and helped enormously with her comments and suggestions. Caroline Webster read a later draft and commented usefully.

Keen that my portrayal of life inside should be authentic, I consulted widely with people working in or with the prison service. Kate Beswick put me in touch with Neil Beales, then Deputy Prison Governor at Huntercombe Young

Offenders Institution, who was especially helpful. Valuable insights came from Gemma Baranowski, Young Persons' Support Worker, Camden; Dave Lloyd Jones, Director of the No Way Trust; Ronald James HMPS, who arranged for me to visit Aylesbury Young Offenders Institution; Arthur Wilson, formerly Senior Prison Officer at Bedford Prison; Gordon Garvie, formerly Prison Chaplain at Wormwood Scrubs; several young men I met 'inside' and Sarah Robson.

I am grateful to Liz Wickins and Sarah Keenan and their pupils – especially Jessica Harding, Kirsty Gilks and Jamie Gibson; and to John Scott of the Ministry of Justice; and fellow writer, Theresa Breslin, for giving me valuable feedback on the script.

I fully acknowledge all the help I've had from everyone named above, also my editors Liz Maude and Charlie Sheppard, while accepting complete responsibility for my creation. If I have forgotten to thank anyone by name – I spoke to so many people – please forgive me. Like all my novels, *Inside* is a work of fiction, the product of my imagination informed by real life. Any mistakes are entirely mine.

HANGMAN

JULIA JARMAN

'Bullying's no joke! Read this incredible book and take note.' THE TIMES

Toby's heart sinks when he hears that Danny is coming to Lindley High. Danny is different – that's the trouble – and being Danny's friend could destroy Toby's street cred. He doesn't want to harm Danny. He wouldn't bully him. Of course not. But their classmates are not so restrained. On a school trip to Normandy, close to the D-Day beaches where men fought to defeat Fascism, a harmless game goes dreadfully wrong.

9781842706831   £4.99

NICHOLAS DANE

MELVIN BURGESS

They were up as soon as they landed and running like dogs. The rain had slowed to a drizzle for them. There was a shout. They looked back and saw someone already had a leg over the sill . . .

Nick Dane is a survivor. He has to be. When this truanting, troubled fourteen-year-old loses his mother, he is sent to a brutal care home. Intimidation and violence keep order. But worse is the kindness of the deputy head, Mr Creal. For the sweets and solace he offers Nick come at a high price. Soon Nick realises that escape is the only option from a life of such abuse.

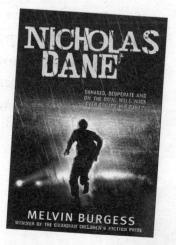

'Harrowing and riveting . . . the psychological insights are rewardingly complex.'
TELEGRAPH

9781842701812   £12.99

THE TRAP

JOHN SMELCER

Johnny pulled the fur-lined hood of his parka over his head and walked towards his own cabin with the sound of snow crunching beneath his boots.
'He should be back tomorrow,' he thought.

Johnny's grandfather is out checking trap lines, but he has been gone much too long. Proud, stubborn and determined to be independent he may be, but he has caught a foot in his own trap and hasn't the strength to free himself. As Johnny worries about him, he is menaced by wolves, plummeting temperatures and hunger. Does he have enough wilderness craft and survival instinct to stay alive? Will Johnny find him in time?

'An unforgettable story. Brilliant!' Ray Bradbury

9781842707395 £5.99

OUT OF
SHADOWS
Jason Wallace

Zimbabwe, 1980s
The war is over, independence has been won and a
new government is in power offering hope, land and
freedom to black Africans. It is the end of the old
way and the start of a promising new era.

For Robert Jacklin, it's all new: new continent, new
country, new school. And very quickly he learns that
for some of his classmates, the sound of guns is still
loud, and their battles rage on . . . white boys who
want their old country back, not
this new black African
government.

Boys like Ivan.

Clever, cunning Ivan.

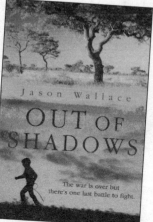

For him, there is still one last
battle to fight, and he's taking it
right to the very top.

9781849390484   £6.99

this is
what I did

Ann Dee Ellis

I always run.
I always run and maybe I am what they say.
I wrote this down and it's supposed to make me feel bette
It doesn't.

Logan has a dark secret too shaming to tell
anyone. He knows too much about the violent
tragedy that overtook his best friend. His family
has moved neighbourhoods to give him a fresh
start, but now he's a target for
the bullies in his school. Can
he summon up enough
courage to own up to the
truth? Or will he let the slurs
and assumptions of the playground thugs
determine who he is?

9781842706770 £5.99